Chapter 1
Sunday, February 5

"WELCOME BACK! ARE YOU READY for some laughs?"

TV Host Sid Caesar bounded from center stage towards the camera like a lion overtaking a gazelle, vibrating with zany energy, pulling crazy, rubbery faces before running to address his guests, who stood near a microphone stand at stage right.

"Ladies and Gentlemen," Caesar continued, "I want to welcome to *Your Show of Shows* a close friend of mine, and his friend."

As Dina watched the video, she spoke the response that came from one of the two guests: "Hey, which one of us are you talking about?"

Before Caesar could answer, the orchestra started playing "Tea for Two," as Alan Bricker and Dominic Delvecchio began a soft-shoe dance. In the beautiful black and white of 1950, Bricker and Delvecchio danced until Dominic called out:

"Stop. Hey," Dominic asked Alan. "What's this I hear about you having another baby?"

"We're not having another baby," Alan answered. "Where'd you hear that?"

"I saw you were planting a tree in the front yard—I thought maybe you're gonna make me a brother."

Dina shifted in place as she watched the video playing on the TV on the wall. How strange, she thought, to make a joke that insinuated—actually, no, plainly stated—that Dominic was supposed to be Alan's son.

He was and he wasn't, Dina thought. The way black and white wasn't black and white. Everyone called it "black and white," but old TV, old footage of nearly lost TV, was usually a grainy mash of gray. Even the shadows came nowhere near black.

While Alan wore a boring, TV-standard tuxedo, Dominic always appeared in a straw hat, striped jacket, and bright pink pants, it was Dominic who drew the eyes of the crowd. They went into a barbershop song:

Meet me tonight in dreamland,
Under the silv'ry moon.
Meet me tonight in dreamland,
Where love's sweet roses bloom.

And then they stopped to bicker more:
"You're always stepping on my lines!"
"Any more complaints from you and I'll trade you in for a sawhorse!"
There again, Dina thought, a reference to wood. Two premises that the audience loved: Dominic was Alan's son and Dominic was made of wood. All of this because Dominic Delvecchio, the sarcastic and outspoken partner of Alan, was a puppet.

Dominic was a small wooden man—sometimes seemingly more of a boy—wearing a tiny version of a barbershop quartet uniform and a tiny straw hat on a tiny little wooden head. His jaw was hinged, and practically everyone knew that he was controlled by some mechanism of Alan Bricker's that most people could only barely understand. And further, every word out of Dominic's mouth was put there by Alan Bricker himself.

Ventriloquist dummies, as a spectacle, have always relied on the art of creating an illusion that stops short of full immersion. The audience is never meant to forget that the doll is truly inanimate, so they can safely enjoy pretending, and never lose sight of the talent of the person behind the illusion. It's a special kind of deceit, the kind that the target can be in

DOMINIC

BY LEE GUZMÁN

A NOVELLA

CASTLE BRIDGE MEDIA
DENVER, COLORADO, USA

CASTLE BRIDGE MEDIA
Denver, Colorado

Cover photo by Yitzilitt/Creative Commons BY-SA 4.0.
This photo has been modified.

This book is a work of fiction. Names, characters, business, events and incidents are the products of the authors' imaginations. Any resemblance to actual persons, living or dead, or actual events is purely coincidental.

on for a time.

They reached the final stanza, Dina remembering every breath before it happened:

Come with the love light gleaming
In your dear eyes of blue.
Meet me in dreamland,
Sweet, dreamy dreamland,
There let my dreams come true.

Applause, then, and the pair bowed.

Sort of a bow.

For a brief moment, Alan Bricker, holding Dominic on his crooked arm, took hold of Dominic's wrist and waved the puppet's little wooden hand. At this moment the strangest thing seemed to happen, which is that the doll lost all of its own inertia. Bricker allowed a collapse of the illusion, so that in the moment, the audience became completely certain that what they were looking at was not a live creature.

"Hey, how's that, little campers?" Sid Caesar shouted. The camera swung over to Caesar, who was hanging out with a gang of kids in the audience. Dina had no idea why the kids were there; were they really here just for Dominic, or would there be another kid-oriented segment later?

But among the youngsters was tiny blonde Gretchen Bricker, the ventriloquist's flesh-and-blood daughter. Gretchen smiled and waved, extraordinarily pretty, a girl who would later become one of the most stunning models in the world.

Dina Maron blinked at the video. She knew it so well that she could even anticipate changes in texture and shadow, and when the cuts would come. She watched the image of the little girl who would be her grandmother, and in her mind, even though already the "Meet Me Tonight in Dreamland" video of Alan and Dominic was starting again, an entirely different video of Gretchen was playing across Dina's memory.

That would be the interview between Gretchen Bricker and Barbara Walters, in which Gretchen summoned up her feelings about growing up with the extraordinarily talented and world-famous Alan Bricker and his dummy Dominic Delvecchio. And what Gretchen said was:

"I hated that goddamn puppet."

The Barbara Walters interview, which was still way before Dina's time, was as clear as day in her mind. It was one of those events that she understood was touted all around the world; if you were watching TV in the mid-1980s you couldn't miss a Barbara Walters special. Dina was too young to have been affected by that, but she had seen the video many times. In her mind she could see Barbara in her high back chair—in her memory it was a peacock chair, but that probably wasn't actually the case. Barbara was always surrounded by orchids and tulips and cast in soft light and possibly even gauze over the camera to give her a kind of Hollywood glow as she sat across from the amazingly beautiful Gretchen Bricker. Barbara and Gretchen talked about her modeling and acting career, and her recent return to mega-stardom with a sitcom that played against type, where the cover girl was now cast as a middle-aged, ballsy newspaper editor. It was a part that employed Gretchen so effectively that the viewer would be forgiven for forgetting that she was one of the most well-compensated models in the world. But the quotation that always stuck in Dina's mind was her answer to Barbara Walters' question about Bricker and Delvecchio. "I *hated that goddamn puppet.*" Dina found herself saying the words out loud and then shifted uncomfortably because her mother heard her.

"What was that, dear?" Dina turned around and saw that her mother Lorelei Bricker was coming into the video room. Mom held a can of air purifier in one hand and her other hand was covered in a dusting glove that she used here and there to wipe off the surfaces. Dina was standing next to the door of the viewing room. They were the only two people in the Bricker Museum, which Dina thought didn't bode too well for the business, considering that it was already five after 9:00 in the morning. Would the museum stay empty all day?

"Mom, do you really need to work today?" she asked. "I mean, it's Monday. Does anybody even go to a museum on Monday?"

Mom waved the air. "If anybody wants to come, I think we should be open. What was it you wanted?" She started walking and Dina followed her through a large foyer area that was actually a connector to the larger building of the museum. The oldest part of the museum was a two-story Victorian house with a garret and a basement, several rooms on each level. But in the 1970s, sales of old Dominic Delvecchio videos in Japan brought the family an influx of money and one of Grandpa Bricker's last major acts was to build an enormous warehouse addition. Thus there in Mujeres, California, was one of the largest private museums in the country, all of it dedicated to the pop culture of America of the 1920s through the 1960s, but all through the very strange prism of Alan Bricker and Dominic Delvecchio.

"I wanted to ask you about the tearoom," Dina said. "Have you thought about my proposal?"

"Oh, gosh." Mom gave a flippant little wave, blowing it off already.

Dina went on, "You could very easily take part of the upstairs, maybe one of the exhibits that people don't visit as much? And turn it into a tearoom." She plunged on, not giving her mother a chance to interrupt. "We're very well situated for it. We're pretty close to the ocean. People could get here quickly. You could rent the space out for sorority teas and wedding rehearsals."

Mom shook her head. "Honey, that's not what we are. You know: we're here to celebrate your great-grandfather's vision and how it shaped American culture."

The grandiosity that ran through Dina's family was absolutely unbelievable to her. She looked around, eyes resting for a moment on an image of Alan Bricker side-by-side with Muhammad Ali, their arms thrown around one another as they mugged for the camera. The shot had had been taken at some fighting rink in Las Vegas, and Dominic Delvecchio could be seen in a chair behind them, though the photo was not arranged so that the eye was drawn to the puppet. For Dina, this made Dominick's presence there seem accidental, but it couldn't possibly have been.

She opened her mouth and closed it, unable to say to her mother what she really wanted to: *None of what you're saying makes any sense. Great-grandpa was a celebrity, maybe even a pretty big celebrity—when Sid Caesar ruled the airwaves!—but he didn't shape the culture, and nobody cares about this museum.* But she looked at her mom and remembered all the hours she had spent at her grandmother's knee, and she couldn't bear to say the words. So instead, she fell back to where she started. "I just think that we might be able to get more visitors in if we started offering a service."

"If you want to start getting involved in the family business, then maybe you can have a little bit more of a say."

"It's not that I don't want to be involved."

"Is that right, Miss Maron?"

"What's that supposed to mean?" Dina asked. But she knew what her mother meant. For years, since high school, even, she had gone by her mother's married name. It was the name of her late father, who had died when she was a child, but her mother said that name as though it were an insult to the Bricker family.

"We absolutely could use your ideas," her mother said, softening. "But I can't run this place and launch new parts of the business at the same time. If you really want to do the tearoom, then come help me. I'm sure you have not just that idea, but *lots* of ideas. I mean, look, I know you think all of this is stupid." It was amazing to Dina that her mother could oscillate so wildly from placating to angry, more so than usual.

Her mother swung her arms wide just as a small bell jingled in the direction that her hand was pointing. Dina heard the muffled sound of people coming through the front door of the museum. Mom dropped her voice as she and Dina headed back that way. It was their strange family way of walking together, whispering angrily at one another, still moving in the same direction.

They walked down the long cobble-stone promenade that divided the imitation American town under one gigantic roof. To their left was a complete American barbershop that had been moved from Alan Bricker's hometown of Saint Louis, to here in Mujeres, California. In the barbershop there was an old marble countertop and stainless-steel chairs, an old barber pole and a full set of razors and scissors. In an enormous mirror, Dina could see herself and her mother moving through. In the back, glinting light off glass, was a real treasure.

"With all of your marketing background, we could really use you."

"Okay," Dina nodded. "Well, then I'm trying to tell you some things that you should try."

"But this is all yours," her mom said, gesturing towards the ceiling, as if heaven itself was her inheritance.

Dina had a sneaking suspicion that this all *might* be hers, but it probably in fact belonged to the bank. She couldn't believe that her mother was making enough money off museum tickets to pay the light bill. But it was certainly possible that the riches her grandmother had amassed and added to the wealth of the Bricker family could keep the lights on in a warehouse museum for decades to come.

Dina couldn't help but look over at a three-foot-tall glass box on a little column in the back of the barbershop next to an antique cash register. Under the glass, in his own little chair, sat Dominic Delvecchio. His little wooden hands rested palms down on his skinny dummy knees, and his little straw hat sat on his painted head. He was in her great-grandfather's death as he had been in her great-grandfather's life save one detail: like a man in a firing squad in an old Carol Burnett skit, he was blindfolded with a pearly handkerchief. There was a label on the glass box that said:

Dominic Delvecchio is sleeping! **Shhhh***!*

"I'm not ashamed of it," Dina finally said. "I just have my own stuff to do. Look, I have to get out of here."

"One of your environmental events?"

Dina shook her head. "A candidate forum."

At that moment, her mom seemed to change completely. They stopped and her mother straightened up. Her mom took it upon herself to straighten Dina's collar. "Well, you've got my vote."

"You know you can come."

"I have the museum," mom responded. They reached the opening section of the museum, where a pair of teenage girls who had just come in were looking at small marionette versions of Dominic Delvecchio.

Dina walked out into the parking lot and saw a couple more cars arriving. So that was good. It might be a pretty good day for visitors after all, but she did the math in her head and knew that fifteen dollars for each of them wouldn't make much difference. She got into the car and sighed.

Chapter 2

DINA STARTED HER HONDA CROSSOVER SUV and pulled it onto Ocean Highway, the main drive that ran north and south along the shore at Mujeres, California. She left the windows down so that she could smell the ocean off to the right over the variety of boutiques and small hotels. The ocean sparkled as she caught slivers of it between the buildings. She could have used her voice to start her phone, but instead she picked it up off the front seat, flipping through it quickly and finding the name SIREN, and then hitting CALL.

Siren picked up after a little bit, her "Hello" sounding immediately like she was distracted.

"What are you doing?"

"You wouldn't believe me if I told you," Siren said.

"Try me."

Siren said, "I'm making a diorama out of all the action figures that I bought for five cents apiece at the Goodwill. It's going to be the Last Supper only with old X-Men figures."

Dina listened to this and thought about it, picturing Cyclops and Jean Grey sitting at the table. "So who's Jesus?"

"Jesus is Nate."

"Who's Nate?"

Siren said, "It's just this X-Men guy with long hair. I don't know. Anyway, he's taller so he was about fifty cents. He's kind of hot." Dina pictured Siren turning over the figurine in her hand. "He has the dainty waist of a ballerina. So what are you up to?"

Dina said, "I'm going to the candidate forum thing. It starts in twenty minutes. I just got back from seeing my mom."

"Oh yeah? So how are things at the Bricker Museum?"

"It's…" she shook her head as she drove. "It's just so preposterous. I feel like I'm talking to people who are in a cult, you know—they really talk about my great-grandfather as though he were a world leader or something. And he was a *ventriloquist*. Do you know that Dominic is in a glass case, like it's a relic? Like it's a holy relic?"

Siren asked, "Okay, so… what's wrong? That doesn't sound like anything new."

"Well, my mom was hinting at me taking over the museum."

"Didn't you say that you had some ideas for the museum?"

"Yeah, but that doesn't mean that I want to actually *run* the place."

"Like it or not, they're your family," Siren said. "They're never letting you go."

Dina reached the parking lot of the Mujeres Community Center. The parking lot was half full. The Community Center was long, low slung, done in pale orange adobe, and behind it were groves of trees and a trail that went down to the ocean. Dina was thinking again about the museum and wondering how in the world her mother was paying to keep it open and whether Mom would have any retirement money at all. She remembered that her friend was still on the line and said, "Okay, I gotta get into this thing."

"I don't understand why you don't want me to go," Siren said.

"It's just going to be boring," Dina said. "You wouldn't like it."

"Well, I have a surprise for you." Dina heard the slamming of a door and then looked across the parking lot to see her friend getting out of her own Volkswagen Rabbit. "I was actually working on the diorama in the front seat of my car," she said, talking into the phone. Siren's hair was done up in bright blue with ponytails, a look that made her seem like an eighteen-year-old instead of the thirty-five-year-old Mexican food waitress and found-art master that she was.

They met up with one another in the middle of the parking lot and walked with locked arms into the Community Center. When they reached the auditorium, they could see that it was half full, which wasn't bad. The stage was set up with a dais for the moderator and long tables for the candidates, the usual microphones and donated water bottles in place. Siren gripped Dina by the upper arm and whispered. "You cool?"

"I'm cool."

The event started up once the candidates for City Council were in their places and the moderator introduced her, reading the bio (BA, JD, civic work, etc., etc.) that she had submitted. The moderator in this case was Terence Fisher, director of the Mujeres Library system. Today, there were four candidates who collectively were running for two at-large seats. Two men, two women; all of them local business owners, plus Dina, who was a local consultant. Among the others, there were two boutiques and one restaurant, while Dina's environmental consulting firm had been building for several years. It was a practice where whenever somebody wanted to plan a building, they would come to Dina to consult with her on how they were both most likely to protect the environment and also most likely to receive all their approvals as they negotiated the complicated rules and regulations of Southern California. The candidate forum was a low-key affair, because to be honest, there wasn't much difference between the four people. All of them were white, all politically moderate, all associated with hanging out with the rich. Everything was going fine until Trent spoke up.

For a moment, when Trent Williams approached the microphone in the middle of the audience, Dina allowed her mind to pretend that she didn't know him, and she tried to see him as a stranger. What she saw was a scrawny man with a slightly receding, graying hairline. Not unattractive, particularly. He was dressed better than she remembered, in that he wore slacks and a dress shirt tucked in, with a belt and a jacket so that he looked like another local business owner. Which he was. Then Trent opened his mouth and said, "I just wonder what Miss Maron would know about serving the community when her business is basically a leech."

A polite sort of murmur went through the audience. Dina looked at

Siren in an automatic kind of panic, and Siren actually started to stand up. Dina held up her hand, patting the air as if to say *no, no, it's fine. He's not that crazy.*

But of course he *was* that crazy. She'd seen it many times when they would be driving along or having dinner or sitting and listening to music and drinking wine. It was always like a switch flipped in his mind, and suddenly his voice got sarcastic.

"I didn't quite catch what you meant," Dina said, leaning towards the microphone, trying to maintain her composure.

Trent rolled his shoulders and gestured with his head towards the other people on the panel. "Well, I mean, all these other guys provide a service." He waved his arm with a little bit of waggle in it, which suggested to her that he might be drunk. "I mean, that guy actually has a restaurant that I've been to, and it's pretty good. And those two people, they sell stuff in stores, but what do you sell? All you do is take people's money, just to tell them whether or not their building is going to get approved. And I wonder if maybe you know secretly whether it will. That sounds like a leech to me, and maybe a crooked one."

There were so many different ways that she could deal with this right now. She could smile politely and laugh, look into the audience, and say, maybe, *oh, hey, I don't know if you guys know but this is my ex-boyfriend.*

Or she could be enraged and shout, *How dare you come here and pretend not to know me and to attack my business. All because of what? Because one of your buildings didn't get approved, even though we were together? That's how you thought it should work. All because I had the temerity to break up with you. Which had nothing to do with your building not getting approved. But that shouldn't be more important to us and our relationship....*

But she didn't say or do any of that. She leaned forward and she said, "I like to think that the service I provide is just as important as the electricity that comes into the side of the building and the water that comes in through the pipes. We live in a very complicated state, and I help people navigate it. We have a lot of rules, and I think those rules are important, and I help people deal with them." She covered the mic and nodded her head towards the moderator, who walked over to her. Dina whispered, "I think he's drunk."

Trent remained at the microphone, shaking, gripping it so tightly that his knuckles were white.

The moderator went back to his spot at the dais. "You know, I think it would be best if you caught up with us later, my friend." He pointed towards the door. Actually less of a point and more of an upturned palm, an open-handed gesture as though offering Trent the door.

"What? What the fuck?" Trent staggered back over-dramatically. Or maybe he was really so drunk that he *was* staggering. Dina couldn't tell. "You think that's the way you can treat a citizen?" And now he was slurring his words to the point that you'd have to be a moron not to see how drunk he was. "Who the fuck do you think you are?" Trent shook his finger so forcefully that he threw himself off balance and stumbled against a lady sitting in a chair next to the mic stand. Then the moderator made an almost imperceptible nod, and then there were two police officers with their arms under Trent's shoulders, dragging him back out of the room. He screamed all of the way. Dina watched in horror as her ex-boyfriend, his heels dragging along the carpet, shouted at her, "People don't know you, but I know you. You don't give a fuck about anybody but yourself and you can't be trusted. Don't trust her! You people hear me? Don't trust this woman."

Dina put her hand over her own mouth, as though she had been the one to say it, as though somehow the shame should rest with her. For a moment she wished that she could die, and at the same time she wished that she could use mind powers that only appeared in old comic books and turn Trent to dust. Trent's screams died away, maybe because he was too far away to hear now.

Dina looked at the audience and said, "I'm sorry. I'm sorry."

After that, she wasn't paying much attention as the questions from the audience continued. She let it go by for a few minutes and then mumbled something to the candidate next to her and got up and stumbled out of the auditorium without a word.

Chapter 3

SHE WAS BARELY AWARE OF the world around her as she hurried out of the auditorium, her heels clicking against the tile. By the time she reached the foyer door, looking out the enormous glass windows, she realized that she had no idea where she wanted to go. She just knew that she wanted to get out of the glaring eyes of the spectators at the moment. But now looking out at the parking lot, she could see her ex-boyfriend was still being handled by the police, escorted towards a squad car. They were sitting Trent down on the ground next to the car. One of the police officers was talking to him, waving his arms around in a sort of *aw, shucks* manner, complete with a lazy shrug. Dina had some idea what the guy was probably saying, *you know, look, women drive all of us crazy, am I right?*

She heard one of the enormous doors to the auditorium open and turned to see Siren poking her head out and then coming towards her.

"That was really something, huh?" And then she must have seen what Dina was feeling on her face. "How are you? Are you okay?"

Dina turned back to look at the police, talking to Trent. "I'm fine. I'm just so embarrassed."

"Don't be." She turned Dina back around and put her hand on her shoulder, looking in her eyes. "Everybody in that audience knows who the asshole was, and it wasn't you. Everybody in that audience. They all looked at that guy and realized he was Looney Tunes. And honestly, everybody in that audience probably wondered if you're safe because, Jesus Christ, I've never seen Trent so crazy."

"He's just drunk," Dina said.

"Yeah, well." Siren gestured with her head out the window. The cops were putting Trent into the police car after all. Trent was starting to make a fuss, raising his arms so that now the cops took him. Dina gasped as they shoved him towards the car and bound his wrist with what looked like zip ties, assuming that the world was aligned with what she knew from television shows.

"He is pretty fucking crazy." Siren scowled. "I'm sorry, sometimes I just can't believe that you and he—

"Sometimes me neither," Dina said. There had been plenty of nights when Siren and some date or another and Dina and Trent had hung out together, out for wine or walking on the beach. Now she looked at her friend. "Do you remember him ever behaving like this?"

Siren seemed consider it. "You know, I wanna say no, but there were a couple of times where I could catch a bit of anger coming from him that seemed a little… disproportionate. I did see that a couple of times. But not so much that I would mention it. Did he ever carry on like this when you were alone?"

"Absolutely not. The crazy drunk thing happened after we broke up." In fact, they hadn't broken up over anything overly complicated. It was simply that Dina hadn't been able to get a permit for Trent. And he took that personally. After he wouldn't stop talking about it for several weeks on end, she said that maybe they would do better with some time apart. And a little bit of time apart turned out to be pretty nice for her, and weeks turned into months, and she didn't want to get back together. And then Trent's calls to her became increasingly desperate, and then belligerent, and then, seemingly at random, desperate again. Alternating so constantly that sometimes he would alternate in the space of a single call.

Dina gestured with her head towards the auditorium. "Do you think that hurt me in there?"

"Oh, I think it helped you," said Siren. But they both knew that that wasn't completely true. There were going to be plenty of people in the audience who would watch that guy going off and say, well, she must have done *something* for him to go that fucking nuts. Somebody was going to feel that way. Somebody always felt that way. "Oh my God," Dina said. "I just remembered that the newspaper was in there."

"You mean the Mujeres California *Plain Tattler?* I wouldn't worry about that at all."

"I wouldn't want my mother reading about this." Her mother was very into the idea of propriety and the family keeping up appearances, and that included not even being a victim if you could manage it. As if on cue, her phone began to buzz. "Oh God, my mom is calling me. Do you think it's possible that somehow, she already heard about all this?"

"Oh, anything's possible." Dina held the phone out in front of her and hit the speaker button. "Hi, Mom. I don't know if it's a good—"

A voice she didn't recognize came across. "Ma'am?"

"Who is this?"

The man's voice came back. "Is this Dina? I got it. It says here, it says Dina."

"What do you mean?" Dina asked. "Who is this?"

A pause. Then: "I'm sorry, I'm just, I'm not a paramedic but they're— you're listed under ICE, you know, *in case of emergency.* So."

Dina's chest tightened. "What are you talking about?"

"You should come to the hospital. You should come in real quick."

"Why did you say you're *not a paramedic.* What happened?"

"No, yeah, the phone was here, so I just thought somebody should call. We're at the museum."

"What happened?"

"Your mother was here at the store, and she collapsed."

The next few hours of her life were a blur, a time of people talking to her when she herself was moving in and out, sometimes hearing what they were saying and sometimes looking straight past them or listening instead to conversations of other people in the waiting room who had nothing to do with her at all.

Her mother had been giving a tour at the museum to a group of schoolchildren who had come in. Mom had entered the video viewing room to start the introductory tour DVD, which was mostly a TV special that had been hosted by none other than Phyllis Diller in 1988 about the history of Alan Bricker and Dominic Delvecchio. Her mother had said a part of her introduction and then circled back and repeated the same line again, and then a third time. And then suddenly she wasn't feeling very well. And then she collapsed.

The person who called Dina was a twenty-two-year-old teaching assistant. While somebody else called the hospital, he had picked up Mom's phone and sorted through it, looking for ICE and called Dina's number. But by the time Dina got to the hospital, there was nothing that she could do.

Her mother had suffered a massive heart attack and died within minutes of her collapse.

"What do you do when you lose a parent?" she said to Siren. "I mean, what am I supposed to do?"

When you're a child and your parent dies, you're an orphan, and it was hard to imagine anything worse that could happen. But when you're an adult, there was not an immediate blow to the infrastructure of your life. She made a good living. She had her own firm. She had money from her grandmother and from her mother and when you got down to it, from the wealth of her great-grandfather. So her bills would or would not get paid exactly as they would before her mother had died. But her mother had been somebody she had seen nearly every day of her life, and growing up, she was somebody that brought magic to her. And now a little bit of that magic was gone. It was several hours at home before Dina remembered that she had to call her grandma, and that was when she started to cry.

Chapter 4
Wednesday, February 8

DINA TOOK CHARGE OF HER grandmother during and after the funeral, and the funny thing about taking her grandmother back was that she could lose herself in all the slow business of walking with Gretchen Bricker and helping her into the car and helping her back out. She could throw herself into the business of movement from moment to moment. The work of it all. She didn't have to think about what was coming next, not that anything really was going to come next, because any conversation at this point seemed completely banal. After the funeral, which was already fading out of her memory, she drove Grandma back to the retirement community and couldn't think of anything to say, because what do you say to somebody who has lost their daughter? She searched her mind as she drove in awkward silence through the town of Mujeres.

"Wow," Grandma finally said as she looked out the window. "So what's going to happen now?"

"For you, everything is going to be just fine," Dina said. "Mom left me all the contact information, all the account information for the retirement community. I'll be taking all of that over. It's going to be fine."

"You don't have to talk to me like I'm eight years old," Grandma said. "I appreciate all that. And I know that none of that is easy or exactly what you want to do with your life, so don't take me as unappreciative, but that's not what I'm talking about. I mean, what's going to happen with the museum?"

"Ah." Dina shook her head, gripping the steering wheel. "I don't know what's going to happen with the museum, Grandma."

"Your mom said that you had some idea about turning one of the rooms into a sort of a tearoom, like a restaurant."

"Yeah, yeah, that's possible. Of course, that was just something that I was asking Mom to do, because I knew that she wouldn't sell it. If selling it were a possibility, I don't know if I'd be trying to launch a tearoom. A tearoom is just another word for a restaurant, which is easily the riskiest business that someone can get into. So the idea that you would try to save a failing business with *another* risky business…"

"Well, gosh, Dina, it's only your legacy," Grandma said.

"Okay." Dina didn't want to discuss it. The intense heaviness of the day made her feel so tired that it was difficult to even move the steering wheel. For one of the first times in her life, she felt like the day itself was drenched in mockery. The beautiful sun seemed inappropriate for the moment, the gorgeous trees that they drove under as they turned off the main drive and up the hill towards the retirement community, all of it pleasant. And not even pleasant in a Stepford Wives kind of way, where danger lurked underneath, but simply pleasant and blind to the fact that her mother was dead. Like beauty meant nothing. Like nothing meant anything.

This was what happened to you as you got older. You spent your life trying to build a career, trying to *become* something, trying to mean something to other people. And as you get older you let go of some of your interests and most of your dreams. And then suddenly, you're not here anymore, and none of it made any difference. The sun still shone; the birds still chirped. Everything was still beautiful or not beautiful, whether you were there or not.

Her grandmother was looking out the window when she said, "Did I ever tell you that John Denver recommended we close the museum?"

"What's that? I mean, no, I never heard that. I thought he was a nice guy."

"He was a plenty nice guy," Grandma said. "So this was around the time that they were doing *The Muppet Movie*. And you know, John Denver was *in* that. And Bob Hope and your grandfather and Dominic, of course. And they were all hanging out one night by the pool at the Ritz-Carlton in Santa Monica near where they were filming. I think I was doing another movie and I was invited to drop by. So I come by and there's John Denver out there with his guitar, and I walk by the pool and everybody's hooting and hollering because they know me from the magazines." Grandma was enjoying this memory because there was lightness in her voice.

"And then somebody said, *shouldn't you be working in the museum?* And I laughed and said that the museum was something that my mom was into. That would be *my* mother, who would be Alan's third wife. And John Denver laughed and said you can't have a museum dedicated to yourself. And I think that my father tried to make it clear that the museum was something dedicated to pop culture of the century, but you know, I don't think that meant anything to *anybody*. Even Dad: I think the only time that my father ever really came by the museum was when they finally built the box that they put Dominic into. He seemed to be in awe of that box and the idea that when Alan Bricker was gone, Dominic was going to go into it." Grandma shook her head. "Maybe."

"I'm lost," Dina said. "What do you mean, *maybe?*"

Grandma bit her lip. "When my father was getting really old, there were a lot of preparations he made. And they prepared the box for Dominic, but I know that that wasn't his first choice. But I'm telling you, that entire museum exists because that doll is there. So John Denver was one of the nicest people on the planet. But he didn't understand what the museum was for."

"Okay."

Grandma scoffed. "Okay... I know what a noncommittal answer sounds like. And we'll talk about this more tomorrow. I know you think that the museum is special, but you don't understand what it means. But let's save it for another day. John Denver was a very nice man, but he was wrong."

They reached the circular driveway on the front of the Retirement Center and Dina pulled the car to a stop in front of the building. Somebody in a uniform came to the passenger side door, greeting her grandmother by name. "Hello, Mrs. Bricker! So glad to see you back." The guy obviously didn't know that Mrs. Bricker had been to her daughter's funeral, and Grandma, to her credit, just nodded.

Dina leaned over. "Do you want me to come in with you?"

"No, go back," Grandma shook her head. "Trust me, there's nothing pleasant about it." Dina started to open her own door to walk her grandma in. But Grandma insisted, "I got it. This young gentleman will help." Grandma stepped out and closed the door, and then she turned around, looking across the passenger seat at Dina. "Can you come visit me tomorrow?" That would be Sunday.

Dina nodded without even thinking about her schedule. "Sure."

"Good. We need to talk."

"Of course."

Her grandmother grew serious. "We need to talk about your legacy, about what you're going to do."

"We can talk about anything you want. I have all of that—"

Grandma shook her head. As though she wanted to be a lot more intense about this and was allowing herself a little bit of humor. "No, There's a lot more. I'll let it keep tonight, but we need to talk. I lived up to the legacy, and your mother did too. It's going to come to you."

Chapter 5

THE CONDOMINIUM THAT DINA RETURNED to had absolutely nothing in common with the world of her great-grandfather, or her grandmother, or her mother. And that was one of the reasons why she liked it. Even though it was spectacularly out of time in its own way, there was a lot that she could do with throw rugs and Columbian art to take the edge off. But it was impossible to hide that the condo itself was an early 1980s masterwork of concrete and shining chrome. There was a movie called *Bad Influence* with James Spader and Rob Lowe, where Spader was some kind of finance muckety-muck and Rob Lowe was a smooth-talking con artist, and they move through a world of brightly lit neon and steel that was indicative of Southern California in the 1980s. This condo had shown up in that film, perfectly fit, though the shiny world of the 80s was a world that she had no memory of herself. And even though it was one of the times when her grandmother was at her most famous, it had left almost no imprint on the legacy of her family.

Decades themselves showed ghosts, however. There were posters in the museum from film festivals, conferences, and television specials that Alan Bricker had participated in during that era. She could always pick the posters from the 1980s out because of the bizarre fonts, the hot pinks and bright blues, the random geometrical shapes floating on glowing grids. You could spot the ghosts of the 80s as surely as you could a 1960s poster that would proudly feature a handmade font and plenty of paisley and little bearded hippie cartoons.

Her home was pristine, with just a few tasteful pieces of art and none of it dedicated to the world of Dominic Delvecchio and the barbershop quartets.

Except for one piece: For sentimental reasons that she couldn't put her finger on, Dina kept a store-bought Dominic Delvecchio doll sitting idly in a papasan chair in the corner. If she had children, they would probably pick it up and play with it and try to see if they could make a doll talk without moving their mouths, but instead it was just a visual speed bump. A little man in a little straw hat, little garters on his little arms. When she had first gotten the condominium and put him in the Papasan chair, she had made a point of greeting him when she came in. But as the years had gone by, she had come to ignore it. When she did remember it, she regarded having it as healthy, that she was finally dealing with the presence of the family legacy.

Now, in the evening after burying her mother, she sat at her table and popped open her Mac.

The background image on the computer was a photo of Dina and her mother at the Bricker Museum and it made her throb with pain. The picture came from a few years ago, when the Mujeres Rotary Club had a meeting inside the barbershop exhibit.

It occurred to her there was more of her life inside this computer than out of it. That the condominium showed almost no aspect of her personality, but all she had to do was pop open her Mac and there was the museum and there was her mother.

She was flummoxed to see that she had nineteen messages awaiting her on her dating app. Seventeen of them were from one person. She rubbed her eyes and looked at the top. It was from a guy called Matchstick and he wrote:

Hello, I just wanted to say that I thought that what that guy said at your event was really shitty and I thought I'd send you a note saying that the community is pulling for you.

That made her feel good. But she bit her lip, since she knew that there were eighteen more messages to go. The message went on:

Anyway, I'm a local guy, you may have seen me. I manage the Golden Crown on the beach. I'm 44, divorced, two kids who I share custody of. I hope it's not too forward to say, maybe it'd be cool to get together, because I really admire how you handled yourself and all the things you had to say.

Dina sat back. That really wasn't bad at all. The next message had come 45 minutes later.

Speaking of handling yourself, I'll bet you handle yourself pretty well.

Ugh.
The next message came 20 minutes after that.

LOL

The next message an hour after that.

LOL Is anyone there?

Then another few minutes after that.

Is this what you're really like? Somebody is nice to you, and you walk right past them.

Who was walking? She was driving her grandmother around. She read on in disbelief.
Next message.

So that's how it is. I'm a nice guy and you're not even responding. You don't even have the politeness to respond. I'll bet your mother didn't teach you anything. She must have been a real bitch to make you into such a bitch. Bitch.

Next message.

Fuck you. I hope you get raped and die.

Dina slammed the laptop shut, touching her eyes with her sleeve. *Good Lord, what the hell was that?* She felt like she'd been hit by a train, but also the train had zipped by without her noticing. There was somebody out there living a drama that involved first admiring her and wanting to ask her on a date and now for some reason believing that she was a horrible, evil bitch. And all the while she had been at a funeral and hadn't had any time to deal with any of this.

She opened her Mac back up. She breathed. And finally, against her better judgment, she hit REPLY.

Hey, I'm sorry, I've been out. I was dealing with some stuff.

She didn't know any other way to say that she had been out of funeral without actually saying it, and somehow that seemed impolite, which was hilarious to her that she wanted to be polite to this complete stranger who had just said that he hoped she would get raped and die. To her shock, the message board pinged with an answer almost instantly.

No. Too late. If you can't have the class to respond to somebody who's trying to be nice to you, I got no time for that.

Dina shook he head. *You have no time for this?* You just responded instantly after messaging me all night.

Whatever, buddy. Have a nice life.

He responded to that, too:

Fuck you, bitch.

She couldn't help it. Tears came to her eyes, and she went over and selected BLOCK and closed the app. After a moment, she opened it back up again. Looking at the inbox because there were other notifications. Thankfully, nothing too exciting.

She went to her e-mail. There was a message from the funeral parlor. Pure solicitude, no invoice yet., though that would probably come tomorrow. There was another message from somebody called Jeff Green.

Hey there, this is Jeffrey Green. I'm your mom's real estate attorney. I wondered if we could meet up at your mother's museum to chat about the estate. If you're ready.

Dina breathed. That was what she wanted to do, wasn't it? She hit REPLY.

I'm glad you reached out. That sounds fine. Are you around tomorrow?

She went ahead and set up a calendar item and invited Jeffrey. He would either accept it or not, and then she closed the computer. And held the wine up to see if she wanted to refill it yet. Through the bleary glass she could see the slumped-over Dominic Delvecchio doll staring back at her. She decided she didn't need more. She went to bed at 4:00 o'clock in the afternoon with the glass and her remote control.

Chapter 6
Thursday, February 10

DINA DROVE BACK TO THE MUSEUM and got there at about 8:15 in the morning. The parking lot was empty, and she was annoyed because that was the time that she was supposed to meet this lawyer named Jeffrey, and there was not a single car in the parking lot, not even the annoying Mercedes-Benz that she imagined he would be driving. She got out of her car and walked towards the leafy entrance to the Victorian house. As she turned the corner into the garden, she was shocked to see a man leaning against the wrought iron gate. He was wearing blue jeans and a climbing jacket, and next to him was a hybrid mountain bike with road tires. The man was leaning against the wall and held up a hand in a casual wave. Despite the fact that he had apparently biked here, he was not a bit sweaty or out of breath. It was possible he had shown up very early and had been waiting a long time. He wasn't in absolutely perfect shape, a slender body marred by a protuberant midsection, but he was handsome, with a dimpled chin and floppy blonde hair. He looked to be about forty years old. "Are you Dina?" He asked.

"I hope you haven't been waiting too long." She wanted to ask him, *Where's your sport coat? Where's your briefcase?* Although she knew, of course, that most lawyers hadn't carried briefcases in many years. But she did rather expect a sport coat.

As if reading her mind, he said. "Not at all. I'm sorry to be so casual, but I'm supposed to go on a ride after this, and I figured with it being Saturday morning, we wouldn't stand on ceremony."

"Not at all," she repeated.

"So this is the place?" He let the question hang in the air as he stepped back, and they stood side by side in the middle of the small courtyard with the vines hanging around it, looking up the side of the house. She nodded, pulling her keys out of her purse, and opened the door. They went into the foyer, which was in a pale gold that had been updated about eight years ago. For the first time, she looked at the place with fresh eyes, as though she were going to have to physically carry out anything that she saw. There was an enormous storage bench in the foyer next to a large vanity mirror with a plaque next to it. The plaque said that her great-grandfather had used this vanity in his hotel in New York in the 1930s when he starred in the film *Dummy with My Face*. She remembered that it was a strange comedy about identical men with identical ventriloquist dummies who decided to trade places. Yet another of many variations of *The Prince and the Pauper.*

"Do you know what kind of business the place does?" The lawyer asked.

"I know a little bit. I worked with my mom a lot, and I was even going over some proposals with her."

"Do you have a conference room where we can go over things?"

"Sure. I can give you a tour along the way." The next room on the way to the ticket booth was technically a gift shop and included props and posters from a lot of movies that her great-grandfather had been tangentially involved in, plus various other things like Hollywood maps to the stars. Those were the sorts of things that were impossible to keep up to date, so they were always getting stuck with merchandise that couldn't be moved. There was candy, but of course the problem with candy was that it went bad. Except for hard candy, and to be honest, nobody really wanted that. Besides, Mom wasn't really in the business to run a gift shop. So the place had a certain haphazard feel.

They stepped into the museum itself as they passed the ticket booth. This meant crossing a large dining room, which was done up perfectly to look like a home dining room of the 1930s. Dina gestured around the room as they walked through it. "What you're walking through is a replica of my great-grandfather's home where he grew up in Saint Louis. If you're doing a tour of the museum, you can either start here and then move your way up into the house, or if you're more interested in The Bricker Museum of the 20th Century, then we go through here." Out of habit she used both hands to point towards a door that led to the connector and the larger museum.

Jeffrey followed her, and then she heard him gasp as they walked into the enormous replica of a small town. "Wow."

"Yes, everything that you see here was moved in from some place or another." They passed by a cafe which was not actually a cafe from St. Louis, but that had been moved from somewhere in Iowa.

Dina said, "My favorite thing when I was a little girl was setting off these sensors." She ran her hand past a thin, dusty light in the air that that ran along a railing. "Watch." She swiped her hand again, this time sure to catch the motion sensor.

In the café, mannequins sitting at little tables and came alive, reading the sports scores and laughing about current events. They chattered on about Alan Bricker, who at this point in the narrative of the museum was in high school and had been featured on the radio.

They also talked about the new medium of television and how it would *never catch on*. This joke, "It'll never catch on," which had been used in everything but from *Saturday Night Live* to the Disneyland Carousel of Progress ride, was literally the oldest joke that Dina could think of regarding stories that take place in the past. It was a groaner, and yet ever since she was a child, she had seen people walk through this exhibit, listen to this dialogue spoken by the mannequins in the café, and elbow one another and even repeat the joke. *It'll never catch on.* Television, that was. *It'll never catch on* itself caught on over and over forever. At least that was the case until Dina had stopped going through the museum. Maybe today's audiences would be less gullible, she thought, but somehow, she doubted it.

They passed an entire blacksmith shop brought in from somewhere in Texas. As they went by it, Jeffrey put his hand on the wooden railing, and they looked over to see mannequins that wore vintage blacksmith clothing and were going about the business of hammering horseshoes and beating nails against anvils.

At this one the mannequins read little dialogue bits to one another about what their life was like. It included a mention that they were going to go see the young Alan Bricker, who had such an amazing skill as a ventriloquist that he was sure to be famous one day ever since he had discovered that he loved ventriloquism on a Boy Scout trip.

Over near the Blacksmith Shop was a barbershop quartet, and two members of the quartet were Alan Bricker and his dummy. These dummies were situated in front of a great old Stagecoach that sat in the middle of the building on the handmade-brick street, giving the perfect illusion that they were outside even though they were under warehouse a roof. Jeffrey made sure and swiped his hand wide and the barbershop quartet began singing, *Meet Me Tonight in Dreamland*:

Come with the love light gleaming
In your dear eyes of blue.
Meet me in dreamland,
Sweet, dreamy dreamland,
There let my dreams come true.

Dina found herself smiling and nodding along.

Jeffrey laughed. "This is fantastic!"

Next was the barbershop with another set of four barbershop mannequins and once again a little Dominic Delvecchio dummy in the arms of a mannequin that was supposed to represent her great-grandfather at some point in his adulthood, with beautiful brown hair slicked back. They all wore the same straw hats. Behind them were a couple of big screens on the wall, and Dina touched a button on the counter. The screens came on, silently showing films of the Great Barbershop Tour that her grandfather had done in 1953. There was an image of Alan Bricker meeting up with dancer/director Gene Kelly, the director of a film that they did together that would be nominated for an Oscar for original music. Vaguely, in the back of

Dina's mind, she remembered her mother, or maybe it was her grandmother, telling her that Alan was very upset that he had not been nominated for the Best Supporting Actor Oscar. He had gone out of his way to lobby every member of the Academy who he could get a hold of, even making personal appearances at their schools. And yet it all came to nothing. There was no nomination for Alan Bricker, although Dina really had no idea if he was a good actor or not. She had never seen the film that he had made with Gene Kelly. Nevertheless, there were images of Kelly magically dancing with the Dominic Delvecchio doll.

"Is this the real Dominic Delvecchio?" Jeffrey asked, pointing at the doll in the arms of her grandfather's mannequin.

"Oh, no." She gestured towards the glass box near the back of the barbershop next to the old cash register. She glanced back towards it as she kept watching the wonderful image of Gene Kelly and the dummy. Over her shoulder, Jeffrey studied the box and read the card on the glass: "Dominic is sleeping! Shhhh!..." He chuckled. "Wow. How old is it?"

"I don't actually know. My great-grandfather got Dominic when he was a kid. I think it was just made by some toymaker, so probably it would date back to sometime around the turn of the century."

"It's beautiful," Jeffrey said. "And its eyes are fascinating. But what's with the handkerchief? Is he a bank robber?"

"Bank robber?" Dina looked back, then joined Jeffrey before the glass box. "Huh."

Sure enough, the handkerchief over Dominic's eyes had fallen down to about his nose, so that the eyes were exposed, and she realized that she had not looked at them ever, because they had always been covered. She bent forward, looking closely through the glass. The dummy's head was not as big as that of an actual person, more like the head of a child. Its blue eyes were perfect, so perfect that they created the illusion of being near liquidity. How did they do that? Maybe with some kind of suspended oil? Blue irises with a black center so real Dina felt as though they could dilate any second. She had to look away. "Let me know if he blinks," she said, and Jeffrey laughed.

They made their way to the little movie theater. And behind that was a boardroom. They settled down, and Jeffrey opened a bewildering array of spreadsheets representing her mother's accounts. She asked, "So you tell *me*, does this place make its rent?"

Jeffrey shook his head. "Well, it's not a matter of rent; your family owns this building. But with what this place could get you, you could be benefiting a lot more. I *suppose* you could keep parking it here forever, but…" he shrugged.

"I get it. The museum doesn't make a profit." She raised her hands in surrender. "Why don't you find out what's out there? Just see if we could find a buyer."

He smiled. "Oh, you'll find a buyer for this land."

They headed back out, and she locked up the museum. She watched Jeffrey pedal away out towards the highway. She was already thinking about what she was going to tell her grandmother.

Chapter 7

SHE WASN'T HOME FOR TWENTY minutes before Siren showed up with cartons of takeout from Whole Foods and a bottle of red. "Let me guess, it's perfect timing." Dina simply stepped out of the way, and Siren sashayed in. Dina was just then experiencing the whiplash of having the buzz of meeting somebody interesting wear off just as she got home, to be replaced with a weird feeling of loneliness that made her consider going back to bed. But here was Siren with olives and couscous and wine, so they dragged themselves out to the balcony, where they spent time watching people running on the beach and playing. Dina reflected that you could see the entirety of the Walk of Man, could see families with toddlers, twelve-year-old girls running and walking and chatting endlessly, teenage boys carousing, throwing one another into the surf. Couples on dates, old men with metal detectors, kite flyers.

"You have to wonder about kite flyers. I mean, look at this guy." Dina gestured down below on the beach where a thin gentleman in clam diggers in a striped shirt and curly brown hair wrestled a kite out over the water. "Like this guy got up and said, *I wonder what I'll do today. I'm going to get my kite and I'm going to go down to the beach.*"

Siren sipped her drink. "Do you think it's a way to meet women?"

"It could *totally* be a way to meet women. One of us could be walking along and say, gosh, show me your kite. But maybe it's more that some people reach a point where they're like, I've got to do something that's going to feel a little different today. I'm going to spend a couple hours on something that's not particularly useful, and I'm going to enjoy it. And the real moment of maturity is when you don't care whether you meet somebody else. It's really literally just going to be you and the kite, or you and the bike, or you and the adult coloring book, or you on the park bench."

"You and the bike?"

"That's how this attorney came this morning. He was wearing a windbreaker and riding a bike."

"Oh." Siren seemed to weigh her next question. "Was he cute?"

"Oh yeah. Floppy blonde hair like Julian Sands, except he looked more like a human golden retriever. Older than me, but not by much."

"Mm. Potential."

"Maybe potential."

Siren seemed to think. "But wait, isn't there like a conflict of interest or something like that?"

"I don't think that counts for real estate attorneys. That's more for the kind of lawyer who's trying to keep you out of jail."

"Not that you'd give a shit right now."

Dina fished through her purse and found a pack of Newports, pulling one out and putting it to her lips. Then she realized that she didn't have a lighter, and she got up.

As she went back inside through the glass door, Siren called, "I thought you quit those things like years ago."

"Don't even."

In the kitchen, Dina found an awkward, enormous oven lighter and brought it back out to the deck and used it to light the cigarette. She inhaled the smoke, savoring the heat against the top of her mouth, and then blew it out. "Man, Trent is an asshole."

"I'll say."

"It's just so unfair that I could just be going through my life and this guy can show up and make my afternoon miserable just because—just because he wants to."

Siren bummed a cigarette. As Dina was lighting it, Siren said, "So you're really gonna sell the museum?"

"Looks like it. I'm not getting back into the family business."

"What about your idea about the tearoom?"

"A tearoom is still just a restaurant. No, I think, the age of the barbershop quartet ventriloquist dummy is probably behind us." Dina looked out at the waves and started to sing a barbershop quartet song.

"Which one is that one?" Siren asked.

"That's one that I learned when I was about seven, it's called 'The Sailor's Lament.'"

"So it's a drinking song?"

"It is a sailor drinking song, arranged for barbershop quartets." She giggled. The sun was going down on the beach, on the balcony, on the kite flyers, and Dina reckoned it was going down on the barbershop quartets.

Chapter 8

IT WAS DARK BY THE TIME Siren left. On the underside parking lot on the beach side where they exited the small two-story condo building, the ocean was so loud it nearly drowned them out. As Siren put her bicycle helmet on and got on her own bike, she shouted, "Text me in the morning!" She waved her handlebars back and forth. "Do you think there's a problem with drunk biking?"

"I don't know, how drunk are you?" Dina asked.

"I think I'll do okay." Siren began to peddle and circled around the parking lot a couple of times, wobbling and saying *whoah* a few times as she struggled to get her bearings. And then she headed off in the direction of her home as Dina walked back towards the front of the of the condo building.

Something scraped hard against a metal garbage can that was up against the brick wall on the outside of the condo. Dina shrieked and then looked at the can disapprovingly, feeling sure she was going to see a raccoon or something jumping from behind it. But there was nothing. The raccoon, or whatever it was, must have scurried off in the other direction. She looked towards the bushes that ran along the front of the building and saw nothing as she passed them and turned up the stairs to her front entrance.

Once again alone in her condo, Dina found she wasn't sure how to act.

There are some kinds of bereavement that take over the entire body and the pain never rests, even for a moment. And there are others that are slow moving, like a trumpet blast far over the horizon. She wasn't feeling it, yet she found herself circling the apartment, warily, wondering how she was supposed to be acting out her feelings or whether she should just drink some more and go to bed. Was eleven o'clock an early time to go to bed when you're grieving?

There had been a point in her early twenties, when she first got her own apartment, when she had distinct ideas of what would be a good way of spending the evening or what would be a bad one, and she always second-guessed herself. Was it acceptable to sit on the couch and watch TV all night? Or was she supposed to be writing a book? Or was she supposed to be playing intense, cool music? Over the years, it wasn't so much that she had grown comfortable in her own skin as that she had grown comfortable enough that she liked what she wanted to do. But tonight, she could not settle down and she had nothing to do whatsoever, so she paced back and forth like an animal in a pen. It took her twenty minutes to realize that it wouldn't hurt to have some music, and she flipped on her smart TV and launched Pandora and paced some more.

After she got the music going, finally settling on, of all things, the barbershop quartet channel, she opened her computer to find that she had yet more messages from the dating app. One was from the guy who had called her a bitch a few days before. She took a glimpse at what he'd written and immediately deleted the whole conversation. And then suddenly she thought better and undeleted it and blocked the user. *Then* deleted it.

Another message, this from somebody named Scott.

Hey Dina, this is one of your neighbors who saw you at the event. You're sure to have my vote.

She replied, *thanks*, and then, as she was about to go back to the inbox, she saw that the message had already been read, followed up by:

So what are you doing right now?

Dina shuddered. *Jesus Christ.*

Another message. This one from somebody called Saint Louis.

I think you show great promise. Are you ready?

Dina slapped her computer closed in disgust. Years ago, she had been in a conversation in college about all the circumstances of sexual harassment and the fact that absolutely, as a young person, she felt flirting should be allowed. Just because you're working with somebody doesn't mean they can't show an interest in you. But there was just something so gross about these guys on these apps, their aggression, that was off-the-charts amazing in its offensiveness. Did it work on anybody? Maybe it did. Maybe it was a matter of your mood, or maybe there were just some people out there who were into that sort of thing. But she wished that she could be left alone without having to deal with it. The last message repeated in her brain. "Are you ready?" Ready for what? What was the stranger called Saint Louis even suggesting?

Her phone pinged with a text message from Trent. *When it rains, it pours.*

Wondering what you're doing.

It dawned on her that Saint Louis might very well be Trent. But what would he be playing at? Why would Trent, of all people, want to be getting back together? Hadn't he hated her when they were together to begin with? Was this a thing where he was hoping that he could catch her at a bad moment, a little bit drunk, just so that they could have sex? She shut down the screen of her phone and set it down, and then it chimed again. Still Trent.

So you're just going to leave me on READ, huh?

She had so many thoughts that she wanted to type, but she finally decided that she would just let it all pass. She typed, feeling obligated, more than anything else.

If there's something you want to talk about, let's talk next week.
She hit SEND.

She could have sworn that she heard a chime right outside her door. She was standing between her bar, which sat just in front of the glass doors with their picturesque ocean view, and her front door. Outside the door were the steps that went down to the front walk. Could Trent be sitting right outside the door? Or maybe down the steps? If he were hiding down the steps, would the chime be heard all the way up here? Maybe. Absolutely. Or maybe it had been her imagination. She opened her phone again and brought up her Ring security camera app.

She had two cameras to choose from, one that showed the front door and the top of the steps, the other showing a view of the bottom of the steps and the bushes. No one outside the door. But sure enough, there was a man standing at the bottom of the steps, just off the sidewalk, mostly obscured by the bushes in the front of the building. He was wearing a baseball cap, and she couldn't see his face very clearly. But on the baseball cap was an enormous orange "T" for Texas. She knew that cap very well. It was Trent.

Her ex-boyfriend paced back and forth, almost completely a silhouette. He took out his phone again and tapped furiously. Dina imagined the little *whoosh* sound as the message left his own phone. And then her phone chimed once again.

Maybe you shouldn't be alone. I thought maybe you would like to talk. I have some wine.

Dina shook her head. Why am I being forced into this conversation?

I'm good, thanks.

Whoosh.

She switched back over to the Ring application and saw Trent get this message, stomping his feet in agitation.

Then, suddenly there was a blur and Trent dropped out of frame behind the bushes.

What the hell? Dina looked at the screen, wondering what Trent had done. Had he simply leapt very fast, and now he was crouching out of sight? Why?

To be out of sight of the cameras. The thought made her shudder. She was thinking of Trent, a bully, a drunk, but not the guy who turns into a true crime documentary—right? She wasn't going to be one of those, right?

But then everyone said that, didn't they?

Dina stared intently, putting her thumb and forefinger on the image and zooming in on the side of the screen where he had disappeared. She thought she saw a shadow, some movement, but she couldn't be sure. *Damn it. Why is he fucking around with me? I just want to be left alone.*

Her phone chimed again on the text. She saw two letters.

HEL

Then she heard a painful yell from below.

So Trent was in trouble? Was he having a heart attack? She had no desire to deal with him, but the idea of having him have a seizure or a heart attack right below her stairs was too awful to imagine.

In her house shoes, Dina padded to the door and opened it, looking down the stairwell. "Trent?" She knew better than to go inspect on her own, but she did anyway, stepping down and down until she reached the bottom of the steps. She heard a scuffle. And when she turned the corner, she found Trent, sure enough, lying on his side and moaning.

She edged around and saw that his mouth was covered in thick blood that mixed with the mashed flesh of his lips such that she couldn't even tell the difference between his lips, his gums, and his teeth. His eyes were rolling in the back of his head, and he was scratching all around him, one dull, repetitive hand clawing mindlessly at the Earth. It took her a moment to overcome her initial shock. But then she shrieked. "What happened? What happened?"

She turned Trent over on his back. There was blood all over the front of his shirt, but she couldn't see where he was hurt, except for on his face.

And then suddenly she realized that whoever or whatever had attacked him, whatever dog or animal or insane maniac it was, might still be here. And she turned around, looking across the street. Cars went back and forth beyond the small expanse of grass to the ocean highway. She heard Trent moan something that might have been *help*. She didn't have her phone, she realized as she patted her pockets. She ran back up to the condo, her house shoes clapping against the steps. She found her phone sitting on the bar and dialed 911.

"911, what's your emergency?"

Dina rattled off the address. "Something's happened to my ex-boyfriend. He's downstairs and I think somebody attacked him."

"Is he breathing?"

"Yes." Sometimes the ambulances around here could be slow because there weren't enough of them. Her car was right here… "I'm going to take him to the hospital." She slipped on a pair of tennis shoes, grabbed her phone and her purse and her car keys and ran back down. She crouched by Trent and said "Okay. Okay. I'm going to get you to the hospital."

She ran to her Honda and brought it back around the corner of the building in an instant, stopping it on the grass right next to where he lay. She got out of the driver's seat and ran around to where Trent was and then realized the passenger door in the back was still locked. She cursed and ran back and unlocked it. Then she dragged him into the passenger seat, fully aware that she was smearing blood all over the place. She had to pick him up by the shoulders, face-to-face, push and slide him in his woozy unconscious eyes only semi-focused on her. "What are you doing?" The words were slurred and without conviction.

"I'm taking you to the hospital." She folded his knees in, and he fell over in the back seat—good enough to just leave him there. She ran around to the front and started the car, heading out to Ocean Highway for the fastest possible route to the hospital.

Chapter 9

SHE HEARD TRENT MOAN WITH A wet, sickening sound in the back seat. "What the fuck, what the FUCK," she called back to him. "God damn it, Trent—what were you doing? I'm getting you to the hospital, you son of a bitch. Don't you understand? I wanted to be alone. My mother died, God *damn* it." Where was the hospital? She was trying to think where it was and then she saw a directional sign: HOSPITAL ROAD with a helpful arrow. Then she realized she was catching a yellow light and sped through just as it turned red. Another car screeched to a halt and honked madly. She called out, "I'm sorry, I'm sorry." She looked back at Trent again. "You see, we're going to get into a goddamn accident."

There was another hospital sign a quarter mile after that. She hooked a slippery right and headed upward into the hills. She remembered this neighborhood along the way because there were some gigantic houses where she had held fundraisers for the Environmental Action Group of Orange County. She could see the hospital complex about two miles away, shining like a city of the future. Before that, there were a number of soccer fields, and before that, a lake. Not a very big one, a man-made lake-reservoir that had been built in the 1960s and people still water skied on, a fact which had always baffled her when she was younger, seeing as there was already the ocean nearby. But of course, her education told her that it had everything to do with diverting water, and almost nothing to do with recreation. She reached the edge of the lake and started driving across the four-lane bridge. Trent said something she couldn't hear, and she heard a bump in the back. Then she heard a weird kind of clacking sound. *Clack-clack.*

"You're going to be okay, okay?" She had to stop herself from letting the habitual pet name of *baby* escape her lips.

He didn't deserve to be called "baby" anymore. She was supposed to be at home listening to Pandora and trying to be a sophisticated version of herself like she read about in Buzzfeed lists. She heard the clacking sound again.

Clack. Clack. Something was moving in the back seat, rumbling against the chair. Dammit, Trent was trying to sit up. "Don't move, just stay where you are," she called. As he rustled and moved more, she looked up and in the rearview mirror and gasped.

Staring back at her, in all his uncanny glory, was the straw-hatted head of Dominic Delvecchio.

Dina shuddered as she gasped, jerking the steering wheel to the right. The car slammed into the concrete embankment and skirted off of it, sparks flying.

She couldn't have seen what she thought she did. Somebody in the opposing lane honked at her, as though she was about to run into them, and she swerved again back into the center between two lanes, another car zipping around her. A wooden hand landed on her shoulder. *This isn't happening. This can't be happening.*

But then next to her head slowly came the cotton sleeve of Dominic, the garter on his arm. She wanted to scream, but she had to keep control of the car. *Oh my God.* She wasn't sure if she was saying that out loud or just thinking it. Dominic was crawling into the front seat, moving over the controls in the center.

It seemed to leverage itself and *flow* into the front seat. Once there, the dummy swiveled its head around as it sat with its knees drawn up against its chest in the front seat, its straw hat tilted back so that some of its reddish hair, which was painted wood, was visible. Its eyes were wet and real, and its wooden mouth opened wide. It hissed as it started grabbing at the steering wheel. Dina tried to bat it away, hitting the dummy hard with her forearm. It slammed against the dashboard. When it did so, its little legs swept underneath and down into the floorboards, where it whipped around and crouched again.

What amazed her most were two things. First was that as the dummy jumped, it appeared heavier than it should, like a big dog. Second, it moved with a clarity and dexterity that was absolutely unnerving. It tilted its upper back so that it could look at her, and then it lunged, grabbing with its little fused fingers for her neck. One of its wooden hands wrapped underneath the seat belt. It was so close that it was almost nose to nose, and then it tried to bite her lips. It hissed and clacked its mouth together, *clack, clack,* smacking at her.

Dina screamed and tried to hit the brakes and somehow missed them, and then the car swerved offroad, bouncing madly. Through the windshield, she could see the ground blur outside amid the flicker of lights. She finally hit the brakes and for a moment she thought they were going to flip over, but the car spun in the mud and then she was headed backwards. She felt herself slam against the driver seat and seatbelt as the car smashed into the water. There was an explosive sound, and an airbag came out of nowhere and smacked her in the face and all went black.

Chapter 10

THERE HAD ONLY BEEN A FEW times in Dina's life when she felt she
was in her body but disconnected from it. Once when she was climbing with
a group of students from college, she found herself just a few feet up a cliff
and completely out of her element. And only when she was falling did she
realize that she had no business hanging out with these people: joking with
them in an SUV on the way they did not bestow on her any of their expertise.
She scrambled for a foothold or a fingerhold and saw clay and rock pull
away. At that point she was both in her body, grabbing for purchase, and
outside of it, amazed at the situation. When she hit the ground, it knocked
the wind right out of her and she could barely breathe, but she wasn't hurt at
all. Outside of some bruises on her shoulders and the backs of her arms, she
had been lucky.

She was floating outside her body once again as the car hit the water.
All the insane images of the thing that had been trying to grab the steering
wheel from her bounced around in her head as she jostled in the car. The
airbag floated away from her face, and she realized that the car was filling
up with water. The water was around her legs and the car itself was sinking
into the top of the lake. She could see through the windshield up ahead where
cars were passing back and forth on the highway. She noticed that one car
had pulled over and the front door of the car was opening. There was water

on her hood now, the dashboard flickering out. She screamed and fought to get her car door open, but it wouldn't budge. The car sank further, the water up now up to her breasts. Distantly, she remembered something that she had seen, maybe in a made-for-TV movie or maybe on an episode of *Rescue 911* where William Shatner taught you what to do if you were in a plane crash or something like that. The car was filling up with water, and she realized the only way she was going to get the door open was if she waited for the car to fill up completely. She couldn't do it. She pounded on the window and tried to get it to open. She pounded on the door. The water was up to her shoulders. And then it was around her face. She looked around, suddenly remembering the dummy. Where was it? Where was Trent? Was he still in the back seat? And then she heard a thump and saw that it was Trent's arm bumping against the roof of the car with the rising water.

She took in a great breath of air as the cavity in the car closed off. She pulled the car handle and the door clicked open, swaying out slowly into the water. She could see next to nothing. She started to move, and then something had her by the shoulders. She screamed, losing all the oxygen she had been holding in her mouth, losing it all in a great cloud of bubbles. And then she realized what was holding her was her seat belt. She scrambled as the air in her mouth grew stale. And she heard it click and open and she pushed off, swimming in a pair of basketball shorts and a tee shirt and tennis shoes. Swimming until she popped her head above the water and coughed. There were people on the shore pointing at her, and she started to swim towards them.

What had happened to Trent, all that she had seen, remained behind her at the bottom of the lake. She swam and doubted, perhaps even intentionally, every moment of it.

Chapter 11

DINA HAD NEVER PRACTICED CRIMINAL LAW. In fact, she hardly used her law degree at all, although it came in handy occasionally in her career as an environmental expediter. She had never once *wished* to practice criminal law, because it was specialized and thankless, and in fact, she knew about as much about criminal law as anybody who regularly watched episodes of *Law and Order*. She had been to law school, so maybe she knew a bit more, but even in law school she relied on episodes of that show to get her through criminal procedure exams.

The one thing she had known since the very beginning was: *absolutely do not talk to the police.* The police, her criminal procedure professor had explained, "are not your friend." You might be a taxpayer, and you might even believe from a policy standpoint that you tend to agree with the police and the things that they do, but if you should find yourself seated across the table from a police officer or, God forbid, in handcuffs, the first thing that you should do is ask to see a lawyer. The second thing you should do? *Shut up.*

She wasn't very good at that at all. When the police showed up, she told them that she was racing her ex-boyfriend to the hospital and that something that surprised her from the back seat had caused her to crash. That was what she said: something surprised her from the back seat. She didn't want to say what she had seen, the thing with wet eyes and the clacking mouth and the straw hat of a barbershop quartet singer. She couldn't say any of that.

The police officer shined a light in her eyes on the side of the road. "So your boyfriend was in the back seat?"

"Ex-boyfriend," she had said.

"So you were driving your ex-boyfriend to the hospital? And he attacked you from the back seat?"

"I don't know, I don't know if he did or not. I think it was somebody else, or, or an animal."

"An animal?" Incredulousness crossed the police officer's face. "Why would you think it would be anything besides the ex-boyfriend that's laying in your back seat?"

She tried to think but couldn't think fast enough. "He was really injured."

At that point, the cop threw her a break, which he didn't have to do. "Are you asking for a lawyer at this time?" And she said yes. She had to repeat it only once, just for clarity, as she dripped water all over the table. "I just want to talk to my attorney."

There was only one that she could think of calling.

When Jeffrey showed up at the police station, he didn't look like he had the other day. Gone were the blue jeans and the climbing jacket, replaced with chinos and a sport coat and a tie.

"I think that's good enough," he said when he came to the doorway. The police officer that was sitting with her went out into the hallway and talked to Jeffrey for a few minutes. She heard them raise their voice for a little bit but couldn't tell what they were saying. It didn't sound like a serious argument. She thought maybe for a minute they might put her into a jail cell and have her sit there for twelve or twenty-four hours until she could be arraigned. But after a moment, Jeffrey poked his head and he said, "Hey, Dina, I think you're okay to go."

She got up and followed him into the hall. She wasn't quite sure what attitude to take, and so she walked in silence for a little while. And then finally Jeffrey said, "So what made you decide to call me?"

She looked up at him. "Well, we just met, so I figured it was impossible for me to shatter your image of me."

He smiled as they kept walking. "It's possible, but I don't think this will do it."

"So what's going to happen?"

He cleared his throat. "So, they'll probably call you when you're back at your apartment. But I don't think you're going to be arrested. Honestly, I don't think anything's gonna come of it. I read the officer's notes from when he talked to you by the lake. You found your ex-boyfriend. He had to go to the hospital."

"Right. I mean, it was bad. It looked like something had bitten his lips off."

Jeffrey grimaced. "I guess we'll find out when they drag the car. Anyway, something attacked you from the back seat, presumably that was your ex. Maybe he was in shock and acting unconsciously. Because of his injuries."

"Well, like I said."

"And it was dark, and you were in a hurry, and there was no way for you to know exactly what you saw."

"Okay." Dina understood. Whatever weird thing she had said about what had attacked her, there was no way that it was going to be spoken about soberly. She tried to think back to the accident. To see the little wooden hands grabbing for the steering wheel. But already it seemed like a dream, like it hadn't happened. It was two o'clock in the morning and she was exhausted. The exertion and the adrenaline had taken all her energy right out of her. But there was such kindness in Jeffrey's eyes that she wanted to say, *Let's go find a Denny's and get some coffee.* But instead, she yawned.

He walked her to his Lexus SUV and drove almost in silence until they got to her condo. She got out and then leaned on the passenger side window. "So I guess you'll call me?"

"Oh, yeah," he said. "We've got lots to talk about. You have to decide whether you're going to sell the museum."

Chapter 12

AS JEFFREY DROVE AWAY, SHE PUT her foot on the bottom stair to go up to her condo, and then stopped. What was she thinking? What she had been taking for granted that she had seen, now that she got down to it, the *creature*, the Dominic that had come out of the back seat—what it must have done to Trent, what it tried to do to her—none of that was possible.

No way.

Except, except.

She was standing there with her keys in her hand, and she realized that she wasn't ready to go back to bed after all. Her body was suddenly alive and awake because she had a question that she wanted answered. She pulled out her phone, thankful once again that it was water resistant. She called an Uber.

When the Uber arrived, it was a long-haired man with a mustache. He was polite enough, and she got into the back seat, pulled toward the tiredness that still demanded she succumb to it, but then she came awake once more when she saw the gymnasium-sized Bricker Museum. The Uber pulled into the lot, and she got out, the cool wind hitting her face. She reached the courtyard and let herself in, making her way into the gift shop and past the video room where her mother had collapsed. Through the section of the old house and then into the larger building, the fake city within the walls.

Past the blacksmith shop with the mannequins. To the barbershop and the glass case.

She turned on the lights just to know for sure. But even in the dark, she could tell.

The case was empty.

As she got closer, she could see that the back of the case, which was made of two sections of cardboard, had been bent back. And the doll had been removed, although already the truth was bubbling in her mind that the doll had somehow removed itself. It made no sense, and yet there it was. She turned around from the case, looking in the giant mirror. Then a barber pole next to one of the old chairs began to turn, spinning as music played over the loudspeaker. It was Bricker and Delvecchio's favorite song:

Meet me tonight in dreamland,
Under the silv'ry moon.
Meet me tonight in dreamland,
Where love's sweet roses bloom.

Her blood ran cold. There was nothing normal about what was happening here. She heard something scrape across the floor, like a chair being dragged. The barbershop was full of shadows, dimly lit by reserved right lights high above the promenade. She faintly saw her own reflection in the wide barbershop mirror. She turned around to look at the barbershop quartet mannequins, including the Dominic Delvecchio mannequin that was in her great-grandfather's mannequin arms. Something rattled. She turned the barbershop lights back on.

She looked at the Dominic Delvecchio doll in the mannequin's arms. Its eyes were plastic. This was one of the toy store versions like she had at home. It didn't have the perfect wet eyes of the real one, like the one that she had seen in her car. Even though seeing it in her car in the first place was crazy, even though there was *no way* it was there on its own. And just then, from behind the back of the mannequin of her great-grandfather, a shape rose, slithering up and perching on her great-grandfather's shoulder.

The real Dominic Delvecchio's wooden head swayed like a cobra's over its white shirt with garters and pink pants. Its arms wobbled like clothed gelatin, its little wooden hands floating freely.

"You're not here," she said.

Its eyes were wet and gleaming and somehow mirthful. It opened its mouth and rattled at her, *ack-ack-ack-ack-ack*, and then the creature jumped. Dina turned to run, smashing against a barbershop chair on the way out to the cobblestone promenade.

The thing landed in the doorway of the barbershop, falling into a heap and then gathering itself up again. Again Dina got the sense of it being something like a snake wrapped in the *suit* of a ventriloquist dummy. Smashing down and then stretching itself up, it coiled its legs beneath itself, and with a hiss and a rattle, launched itself at her. She smacked at it, sending it sliding, and it landed on a long wooden counter that could easily have been the saloon bar of an old Western town.

At the end of the bar was a glass jar full of blue barbershop cleaning liquid. Decorative, but absolutely real. The liquid probably had not been changed out in fifteen years, but it was still full of long pairs of scissors and combs. The dummy coiled itself again, and then rolled its body until it reached the glass jar. It reared back and smashed the jar with its wooden head. Blue liquid flew everywhere.

Just outside the door, Dina didn't wait to see what would happen, but turned and bolted down the promenade. She zipped past the exhibit for the Old Rooming House, which had a "self-playing" piano in it. As she passed, her shadow set off the sensors and the piano began to play. The mannequin in the drawing room began to rock in his chair and talk about the amazing talent of Alan Bricker, the big star of the town who was going into Saint Louis that weekend to audition to be an opening show at the State Fair.

Something shot past her, and the dummy landed in a heap in front of her and then rose up like a cobra, rattling, the rattling more like a hum because in of its wooden teeth the dummy gripped long pair of scissors. It jumped for her, and she felt its legs wrapped around her neck. The dummy stabbed at her before she had time to realize what was happening. She bent her head to the side and the point of the scissors swiped right over the top of her ear, grazing her skin and drawing blood. She grabbed at the creature's head and felt the scissors impale her palm. She swiped sideways before it could get much purchase. Dina screamed without hearing herself scream, managing to get her hands around its head this time, and threw it. It spun end over end, flipping into the exhibit of the drawing room, landing in the lap of a Whistler's Mother-style mannequin in a rocking chair. For a moment, the dummy rocked in the old lady mannequin's lap as she read from the script about how everyone really loved Alan Bricker and that amazing dummy of his, Dominic Delvecchio.

"You are not real!" Dina screamed. The creature, for she could only think of the dummy as some kind of creature now, coiled itself in the old lady's lap and then rose up, wrapped its cloth arm around the mannequin's head, and ripped the head clean off. Unrolling its arm in a whip-like movement, the dummy sent the heavy plastic head flying. Dina watched head's silvery bun spin towards her, and she batted it away in horror. She watched the head bounce down the promenade and glance off one of the wheels of the old stagecoach in the center.

In Whistler's Mother's lap, the dummy grabbed a pair of the mannequin's knitting needles in its noodle-like arm. The knitting needle wrapped in its arm, the dummy left the headless mannequin and began to bounce across the floor in a manner that, in a friendlier situation, would have reminded Dina of Tigger the Tiger in the *Winnie the Pooh* cartoons. It wrapped its legs around and coiled them, and then sprung, and coiled, and sprung. As it bounced towards Dina, she fled to the blacksmith exhibit. She knew what she wanted and found a hammer, grabbed it and swung, bashing Dominic Delvecchio just as he came close to her.

It rattled at her, holding the knitting needle, bouncing back and landing on the promenade. It coiled and bounced again as she ran out of the blacksmith shop. This time, the dummy landed on her, wrapping its legs around her neck. It curled itself over her head, and its weirdly wet eyes stared, it's wooden mouth clacking and rattling. For a moment, she was eye to eye with it. Then it swung its body down, keeping its arms coiled around her neck and wrapped its legs around her body. Now she was carrying Dominic Delvecchio like an infant in a Baby Bjorn. It yanked and pulled her forward, grabbing the knitting needle out of its own mouth by wrapping its arm around the needle, and then it *stabbed itself.* The needle pierced right through the dummy's own body and connected with hers. Dina screamed in pain as the needle struck her sternum and she smashed the creature away from herself. She found a park bench where a mannequin that was modeled after her great-grandfather was feeding pigeons with another Dominic Delvecchio doll in his lap. She fell back against the bench, checking her wound. The goddamn thing had drawn blood, but luckily hadn't managed to stab her very deeply.

Ack-ack-ack-ack. It was coming after her again. She ran for the stagecoach and the creature bounced after her, but this time she was ready. She waited for it to leap and then she grabbed the demonic thing by the bow tie, spinning with the dummy's momentum. She swung it right into the open door of the stagecoach and slapped the stagecoach door closed. She ripped a pair of leather reins from the hands of the stagecoach driver mannequin. She wrapped the reins quickly around the knob, trapping the creature inside.

Looking through the door window of the stagecoach, she saw the creature glare at her and hiss. Then it began to bash its head against the glass, but she was already running, all the way out, all the way through the connector, through the old Victorian house, through the gift shop. Out.

In the cool of the morning outside, she knew several things. She had seen what she had seen. And what she had seen was smart enough to follow her and be ready for her. It was a creature of mystery and a creature of demonic intelligence.

Dina took out her cell phone and dialed Siren's number.

When Siren finally answered, she sounded groggy. "What's going on?"

"I'm sorry to wake you. I have so much to tell you." Dina looked back at the house. "But mainly I have to tell you, I really want to set this place on fire."

Chapter 13
Friday, February 11

IN ONE OF THE ROOMS OF the Bricker Museum, there was a little girl's bedroom, with a canopy bed and an assortment of Louis the 14th furniture. There were a variety of dolls, and a little dollhouse that was almost identical to the Victorian mansion that created the facade of the museum. In the corner sat a perfectly preserved space-age style 1960s television set. It was rounded at the edges, and it sat right next to a window where you could see a beautiful fake Saint Louis street—an illusion of light and miniature. On the TV screen a whole video collection played, entirely dedicated to the owner of the bedroom, had it been the real bedroom: an image cascade of the life of Gretchen Bricker.

Dina had seen the video collection many times when she was small. She would wait for the moment that the museum was open, and she would come in here and lay around in her grandmother's old room. She would recline on her grandmother's bed with the room's vintage phone to her ear, twisting its seemingly mile-long cord, pretending to talk to her grandmother's high school friends and watch the snowy images on the TV.

The scenes played: Gretchen Bricker, born in 1945, running across the grass, a mass of blonde curls and a little blue coat and matching hat sometime in the 1950s. Gretchen volunteering at a soup kitchen with

Dominic Delvecchio as she clutched a stuffed dog. A cavalcade of one star.

There was a moment in the videos when the viewer saw a young Gretchen clowning around as a guest of the Boy Scout Jamboree. She was standing next to the Honorary Scoutmaster General of the United States, her father, Alan Bricker. Alan wore a Scoutmaster uniform, and in his arm, of course, as always, was Dominic Delvecchio, wearing his usual barbershop quartet jacket and suspenders. Except that this time his hat had been replaced with a Boy Scout cap. In another image, Gretchen was making hot dogs and offered one to Dominic, who laughed mightily, his wooden head bobbing in the arms of her father.

Next on view in the video, there were images of Gretchen's amazing career as a runway model in the 1960s, then as a cover girl and actress.

Later in the video were images of Gretchen as a film star and then when her film career was deemed to be winding up, in the late 1980s, her reinvention as a sexy, middle-aged actress in a well-respected television sitcom where she played a hard-hitting journalist so famous that the actual vice president of the United States cited Gretchen Bricker as an example of the fall of culture because her sexually active character on television was unmarried.

Across the span of the space-age TV's video collection, which one could buy as a DVD in the gift shop, Gretchen Bricker went from the ersatz sister of Dominic Delvecchio to a cultural touchstone in American society on her own. Most of this was accompanied by music and most of the music was "The Times of Your Life" by Paul Anka, the license to which had run out decades ago but which went on being used unchecked.

In one of Dina's favorite videos, Gretchen was on with Barbara Walters in one of the most important interviews of her entire life. "I was honored to be part of my father's work," she had said.

As Dina drove her rental car towards the Sun Valley retirement center, she thought about that moment. About Bricker saying exactly that, *honored to be part of my father's work*. And what amazed Dina most was that out of that entire Barbara Walters interview, which lasted for an hour and a half that Dina had only watched many years later after she had changed her name, the bedroom exhibit video had only used a single line from it: "I was honored to be part of my father's work."

Because the rest of it was unusable. At least unusable for the purposes of playing on a television set in the imitation bedroom of the sister of Dominic Delvecchio.

In the interview in the 1980s, there was a moment when Gretchen seemed to stop and stare into the distance. She was no longer in the garden chair, surrounded by lilies, talking to the western world's foremost interviewer. Instead, she was somewhere far away. She paused for a long moment after Barbara finished her question, whatever the question was. And then Barbara started again, and Gretchen said, "No, no, no, I'm thinking. It's...."

She paused again, and then the rest came stumbling out. "The thing to remember is that that doll *lived* with us. It had its own room. Can you believe that? I still run into so many people who don't believe me when I say the doll had its own room. I would get up in the night and go to the bathroom and I would have to pass the bedroom of a doll that my father took with him everywhere. A doll that was world-famous—*world-famous!*" Gretchen punctuated the words with a hard finger. *"I* was world-famous in my twenties. That doll was world-famous when I was *eight.*

"Dominic Delvecchio was there when I had to get my tonsils out. It came to the hospital. And my father was sitting there by my hospital bed, and he knew better than to use that voice to let the doll speak. But I saw him sitting there, and I know that it was *everything in his power* not to let that doll speak. I don't think I even thought about it at the time, just... how *bizarre* it was that he brought it there in the first place."

"Maybe he thought it would comfort you."

The pretty ice-maiden eyes twinkled. "Oh, no. No. My father knew that as much as he needed it, I *hated* that goddamn puppet."

Dina parked her rented SUV at the retirement center, which was a term that she felt sure had not existed when she was a little kid. Dina had to admit when she went in that they were much better than they used to be. The facility that Gretchen Bricker lived in took up an entire wing of a large medical center, so that you could leave the assisted living facility and drive around a parking lot the size of a shopping mall and wind up at a maternity ward. The facility afforded Gretchen a two-room suite with its own kitchen and wide areas where she could maneuver depending on how tired she was with her walker, or even with a wheelchair. A young red-headed woman in a nurse's uniform sat at the front desk and smiled as Dina came in.

"Hello!" The name tag on her uniform said TRACY. Dina wondered, as the woman smiled, if her cheeriness was an act that she performed for everybody, or if she really was just that happy to see somebody who was coming in to see one of the patients. When Dina was younger and more cynical, she believed that almost everybody's enthusiasm was put on. Now that she was older, she realized that some of us put on enthusiasm because sometimes wishing can make it so.

She was fully prepared to have to introduce herself, but the woman recognized her. "Hey there, I know who you're here to see."

Dina looked at her watch. It was 9:30 in the morning. "Are they still at breakfast?" She had to admit she didn't know how it worked here. Was it like a cruise ship, were you expected to go to breakfast, or did they bring breakfast to you? Or could you do one or the other?

Tracy said, "Well, some people are still at breakfast, but I think Miss Bricker is over in the TV room."

"Oh, they're watching TV?"

"Actually, I think that Miss Bricker is keeping them entertained."

Tracy got up and walked, gesturing for Dina to follow. As they walked down the hall, she was struck again by how this place was unlike the old folks homes she had grown up around. The paint was nicer; there were flowers everywhere. The doors looked like a fanciful sort of sitcom-set-like near-reality, as opposed to cold steel and Pepto Bismol pink that she associated with hospitals. And of course, it never left her mind that she was still in a *part* of a hospital, but it could be so much worse.

As she neared the TV room, she heard her grandmother's voice, as smooth and silky as it had ever been when she advertised Revlon in the 1960s or in a series of Charlie commercials in the early 1980s.

"Oh, that was at Niagara Falls," Gretchen was saying. "That was when we met Jerry. Jerry Lewis."

A woman responded, as if on cue, "Can you tell us a story about Jerry Lewis?"

Gretchen smiled. "Oh, well, do you want a clean story?" Everyone in the place shook with laughter. Dina's grandmother was in her element. As Dina entered the TV room, she saw that Gretchen had not been so gauche as to literally take a chair next to the television, but rather was off to one side but subtly arranged so that she was addressing everyone else in the room and all the other residents were rapt with attention. Dina wondered how this Q&A session had gotten started. Surely it wasn't something they did every day. She entered soundlessly, but Gretchen immediately found and saw her. And though Gretchen's mouth was still telling a story about Jerry Lewis that was more or less clean, the wheels behind Gretchen's eyes were already turning.

Chapter 14

"SO TELL ME WHAT HAPPENED," GRANDMA said when they were back in her elegant suite.

"Before that," Dina answered, "tell me how you're doing."

"About as well as can be expected."

"When I saw Mom, she was healthy. We argued. That's the last thing that happened before…" She was shocked to suddenly have to dab tears out of her eyes; they snuck up on you like little traitors.

"Oh, honey. Nothing you could have said to your mother about running that museum had anything to do with her having a heart attack. I'm sort of shocked that *I'm* still around."

Grandma hugged her, and then after a moment she said, "You didn't happen to smuggle in any cigarettes?"

"No, I'm pretty sure they're against the rules."

"Yeah, well, as long as we're taking *that* seriously. So what happened?"

"I don't know if you're going to believe it. I don't know if anyone will believe it, but I have to tell somebody." She stopped and looked at Gretchen, who had changed her affect completely. All the mirth was gone and replaced by cold steel.

"You saw it."

"You're talking about the…"

"I'm talking about Dominic," Grandma said.

"I didn't just see it—it attacked me. *Twice.* "

Grandma reared back her head in shock. Whatever she had meant by *you saw it* hadn't included this. "Jesus Christ! What? So it's not in the box anymore?"

Dina shook her head.

"I thought you were going to come in here and tell me that you saw it moving around in its box. And that its eyes are weird. Which they are. Bizarre."

"They are weird. But that's not it. What the hell is that thing? It moves like some kind of animal."

"Why don't you make some tea," Grandma said.

Dina put the kettle on. Grandma found her place on a sumptuous love seat.

In the kitchen, Dina found a couple of lovely gilt-edged teacups. She remembered seeing them when she was little. They were a gift to Alan Bricker from the ambassador to Chile during one of his tours. "These are the Chilean cups!"

"Oh, those are nice." Gretchen's eyes twinkled as she said it. Dina brought the cups of tea, and they sat down. After a moment, Grandma said, "First, you need to know—"

"You always hated that doll. I know. I saw the Barbara Walters special. But have you ever seen it do this?"

"Not exactly, but I have to tell you that I'm not surprised."

"Do you think it had anything to do with mom?"

Gretchen shook her head. "No. Your mother had a heart attack. I wish that somebody had been with her, but it had nothing to do with Dominic. But he *is* here because of her."

"What do you mean?"

"My father, when he was dying, made me a request. He asked if I would take on his show."

"You mean the Alan Bricker ventriloquist show?"

"Yes." Gretchen shook her head in consternation. "Can you imagine that? I was a supermodel and an actress; I was fighting with the *Vice President of the United States* on the evening news. And my dad asked me this like I was suddenly going to quit my television show and start doing a traveling tour with a ventriloquist dummy—in the late 1980s. I thought he was insane. Or maybe senile. I said to him, I love you. But Dominic is your act. And he said to me, *it's not just an act.* Like I didn't know that, like I didn't grow up sharing a Jack-and-Jill bathroom with that thing." Gretchen sat back and asked, "Do you still know all those old songs?"

"Absolutely, I do," Dina said. "In fact, I know every barbershop quartet song that Dominic sang, and more. It made me very popular in college."

"I'll bet," Grandma said. "I always hated my brother, but I always loved hearing you sing those songs. That's what's so impossible to explain about the love you have for your grandchildren, you'll go ahead and love whatever they love, or at least accept whatever they love. Even if you know better."

Dina was thinking about the time that she spent singing barbershop quartet songs and even trying to get her friends to do it. A painful memory entered her mind, and she pushed it away. All of it was so important to her at the time. And then there came a moment when it wasn't important to her anymore, and she pretended it all wasn't there.

"Anyway," Grandma said, "I told him, Dad, your act is going to be immortal. Okay? People are going to talk about it for the rest of time. Everyone will remember Alan Bricker and Dominic Delvecchio, and the museum is going to make sure of that. I don't need to do your act. And I remember he said to me, 'you think I'm crazy, but I'm not asking you out of ego, I'm telling you. The easiest thing, the easiest possibility for all of us is for you to take over the act. But if not, put Dominic away and cover its eyes, you'll have a fortnight.'" Gretchen's eyes grew wide as she leaned forward. "That was what he said, that I would have a fortnight."

"What did he mean?"

"That's old-timey language for two weeks."

"No, I mean, what did he mean you'd *have two weeks?*"

"I don't know. He was all flustered, but he was full of directions. He said someone needs to give Dominic a voice to care for it. But if that I wasn't going to give it a voice, then I had to put it to sleep within the two weeks. And he told me how. So when my father died not long after, I put Dominic into a box using the instructions he gave me. The glass box in in the barbershop in the museum. I set him in a little chair with his eyes covered, just as he said. I did say a little prayer over him. I put my brother into that glass box and there he stayed."

Dina sat down her teacup. "Dolls don't… I feel insane. Dolls don't just get up and run around. That's not a thing that happens."

"All I know is that that dummy is your responsibility now. I think it would have been your mother's, but your mother knew how much I hated it. In any event, your mother's dead, and now the dummy is looking for you. You have to take charge of it."

"What does that mean? I'm supposed to become a ventriloquist?" Dina didn't think she had tried ventriloquism since she was a kid.

"Gretchen shrugged. All I know is it wants a voice. So you're either going to have to put it back to sleep by covering its eyes, or you can decide to be attached to it. Or…"

"Or what?"

"Or it will kill you and get away, and I'm not sure it's a doll anymore at that point."

"Okay," Dina said flatly. "So what can I do to this thing?"

"Got me," Gretchen said. "I just put it in a box and covered its eyes like my dad told me to. And I was the rebel."

Dina thought about the creature not acting like a ventriloquist dummy so much as a snake being driven around by a wooden head in a straw hat, coiling itself and leaping, bouncing like Tigger the Tiger. Grandma looked very tired.

"You need to rest."

"Yes… But I want you to know. You've done really well. I'm so proud of you. I don't care if you changed your name, I want you to know that every rebellion you did, I did back in the 60s, so it's okay. But this thing is going to be your responsibility." And then Gretchen the supermodel went to lay down.

Dina walked back to the rental car, trying to decide what she was going to do next.

Chapter 15

DINA FOUND HER RENTAL CAR AND threw her backpack into the front seat. Sitting there for a moment, she looked across the parking lot, her knuckles on the steering wheel. She was reminded of all those parents who showed up at the county meetings whenever she was making a presentation about the environment. All of these people would say, *you know, people don't understand how simple this is.* And then they would lay out an explanation for whatever the problem was whether it was Dina's topic or school truancy, or whether or not to charge kids when they came to school without lunch money. What she had realized was that for every complicated question, there was usually a simple answer that was wrong. Dina had a complicated question. There was a homicidal ventriloquist dummy trying to kill her. There was a complicated answer that her grandmother had come up with that involved that she needed to "take charge of it."

Dina was pretty sure that this time there was a simple answer that was right. There was no way she was going to take charge of a doll and cover its eyes or whatever the hell other magical things she was supposed to do. She was going to get rid of it.

She pulled out into the little sun dappled road that led towards Ocean Highway, moving slowly with every motion, thinking. She was going to the museum before she actually really decided it, but by the time she was entering the parking lot, everything she needed to do was playing out before her eyes.

In the lot of the museum, driving through the shade of the trees that obscured the Victorian, Dina felt her chest tighten with emotion. God, her mom was devoted to this place, and at this time of day, she could see why.

She parked her car and sat there a moment staring at the house and the great warehouse attached to it. After a moment the feeling of grief passed like a receding wave, and she got out, taking her purse with her. Outside the car, the traffic sounds of the highway mixed with the wind. She didn't bother locking the car doors. She was only going to be a moment. Honestly, in this town she could probably leave her keys in the car.

There was a coffee shop across the street, Heatherton's, founded in 1976 by Joey Heatherton the actress. That would work. Dina crossed the parking lot, then jogged over the sidewalk and grass and the street, sparse traffic giving her wide berth. Inside the café, the blazing sun gave way to dim light and she blinked to try to see. Inside was wall-to-wall 60s models, Joey Heatherton taking up most of the wall art, but Dina could spot Twiggy, Jean Shrimpton, and of course, in a seven-foot poster, Gretchen Bricker in a sheer robe on a balcony somewhere in New York. It was ravishing; Dina had been in here before with Grandma, who had gone out of her way to let everyone know how thoroughly embarrassed and *shocked* by the image she was.

Dina got a coffee with two Splendas to go. She had killed enough time.

She headed back across the street to her car, opened the unlocked door and threw her purse in the passenger seat. She put the coffee in the cupholder and grabbed a can of mace out of her purse just in time to catch the damn puppet lunging out of her back seat at her.

The little bastard had crawled into her car the moment she was out of sight. Of course.

It ack-ack-acked at her, and she sprayed it right across its weirdly wet eyes.

The dummy hissed and flapped in the front seat, rolling into the floorboard with her purse. She grabbed a duffel bag from the back seat. It came for her, biting at her fingers, but she was able to grab it by the neck.

It coiled itself around her arm and she sprayed it again, stuffing it into the bag. It fell in among a set of workout clothes and she zipped the bag closed. She ripped her own belt off her jeans and wrapped it around the duffel bag, closing it off, cinching it.

Now it looked like a cloth dumbbell, narrow in the middle and wide on the ends as the creature squirmed and bounced on the passenger seat beside her.

She would need to secure the bag some more. She drove until she reached a hardware store and left it writhing in the passenger seat as she walked in, and six minutes later emerged with three long chains and three padlocks.

Then she began to drive again until she reached the reservoir near the hospital. Her whole body vibrated with the need to get this done quickly.

She parked in a little parking lot next to wooden railings where seagulls darted all around. She looked out across the bright morning at the reeds that swayed along the edge of the reservoir. She gauged about where the water got deeper. She opened the passenger side door, pulled the duffel bag out and laid it on the ground.

She wrapped the chains around the duffel bag, tightening it, and finally locked each of them together. She was no expert, but this seemed pretty good. Then she got back in the car and drove back to the bridge, where she had lost her first car just a night or two ago.

She spent less than ten seconds throwing the duffel bag into the reservoir. She stopped to watch it sink, and then she got back into the car and pulled back into traffic.

It was 10:30 in the morning when she pulled off into a fast-food restaurant parking lot a few miles down the road. She took out her phone and she realized what she was doing—acting like everything was normal, forcing her day back into a recognizable reality. She scrolled through her calendar. To her great relief, she was not missing a meeting at this moment, and since she hadn't set up any consultations in the past few days, she could afford to kill the day. She thought about really stretching things out, maybe stopping for yogurt or something like that. Then she decided that that was too self-indulgent, and she headed back to her condo. When she pulled into the condo lot, she noticed a police car parked near the curb, about exactly where she had found Trent two nights before. When she reached her front steps, she found two police officers waiting for her.

"Maybe you can talk to us," one of the police officers said. He had curly hair and a mustache and a badge that said KAPLAN. His partner, a scrawnier guy with a big nose and a badge that said HORSHACK, nodded towards the door.

"Am I under arrest?" Again with the criminal procedure she only half-remembered.

"You're not under arrest," Officer Kaplan said. "But we wondered if maybe you could answer some more questions."

She was seated in a small interrogation room once more. Officer Kaplan looked at his iPad where he had been taking notes, and then looked back at her. "So you said that your ex-boyfriend had been stalking you."

"Yes."

"But you were going to take him to the hospital?"

"Yes."

"Why were you going to take him to the hospital?"

"I told you—because I saw him on the Ring camera. And then I saw him fall. And I went down to find him…"

"Why did you go down to check on him?"

"I don't know. It just looked really suspicious that he had gotten knocked out of the screen like that."

"I don't get this," Officer Kaplan said. "The guy is stalking you, so he's on the camera and he disappears from the camera, and you go check it out."

"Yes. Look, he's a *person*, he's not a monster. So…."

"Can you show us the video?"

Dina felt her face grow red. "I'm sorry, I don't pay for the videos to be stored."

"You're being stalked, and you don't pay for the video on your own security camera?"

"Well, when you say it like that, I probably should."

"Okay." Kaplan signaled that he was moving on. "So you found Trent."

"Yeah."

"And he was injured. Can you tell me a little bit about the injuries?"

"I already talked about this; something had happened to his face. I don't know what happened. But I put him into the car."

"Okay, so he's injured, and you put him in the car, so what happens next?"

Dina stopped for a moment and thought. It didn't really matter what she said now, but she certainly couldn't say that a ventriloquist dummy had jumped out of the back seat.

"It's fuzzy," she said. "It all happened so fast. But someone attacked me. I think Trent attacked me from the back seat. Maybe he was delirious. So then we were thrown into the water." *Thrown into the water.* It was an interesting choice of words. She realized she was going to have to rewrite much of her life over the last week and throw it all into the water like the dummy.

There was a knock on the door. Officer Horshack got up and opened it, and Jeffrey stood there. "Hey, guys," Jeffrey said.

"Oh, is this your client?" Horshack asked.

"It *is,*" Jeffrey said. He kept his hands in his pockets like this was all casual. "You know, you guys don't have any reason to hold her. You're not going to arrest her for murder."

"We're thinking," said Kaplan.

"Thinking? What's your theory? That she drove the car into the water and barely escaped with her own life so that she could drown her ex-boyfriend? On the way to the hospital?"

Dina watched Kaplan's eyes move back and forth and finally make some kind of calculus that she interpreted as: *this is too complicated.*

"Okay," Kaplan said. "You can go. But we might be in touch."

Jeffrey shrugged and tilted his head, and Dina got up and walked out into the hallway with him. As they walked towards the door of the police station, he said, "We've got to stop meeting like this."

"We will," Dina said. They stopped just outside the exit. "Why don't we get some lunch, and you can meet a friend."

Chapter 16

AS THE OCEAN ROARED IN THE background behind the Ocean Highway structures of Mujeres, there were signs everywhere of the impending Heritage Festival. Streamers and balloons had already been hung at various places on streetlights and lampposts here and there on the side streets next to the boutiques. Dina spotted parade floats under construction, teams of teenagers working on them. She felt a pang of shame that in the last week, as a city council candidate, she had not bothered to take part in any of these activities or even to internalize when the parade was going to be, or what other activities would be happening at the festival. And even though she had just dumped the ventriloquist dummy that had been stalking her into the reservoir, she was not yet ready to engage with the world. First, she just wanted to engage with the people in her life.

Pedro's Hula Hut was a Mexican restaurant that sat on a Mujeres pier a mile or so south of the marina. By night it was a candy-colored Christmas ornament of a place lit up so brightly that its reflection blazed on the water and was visible from cruise ships miles out to sea. By day it was a wonderful smelling, strange goulash of classic California Mexican and Hawaiian food all munged together by way of mid-century beach party movies. There were silver mirrors on the brightly painted walls and fishnets hanging from the ceiling. Surfboards and photographs of famous surfers and actors going back

80 years.

As Dina found her way to a little table on the pier, she thought about the fact that this restaurant represented a history of pop culture every bit as rich as the one recorded by the Bricker Museum. Alan Bricker had been a Midwestern comedian who had picked up his joke rhythms from the Borscht Belt. The world of the Hula Hut was one of tanned bronze gods and Beach Boys music. Somehow these worlds were parallel and invisible to one another.

When she got to the table, Siren was already there, working her gig as a hostess. Siren gestured towards a chair, and Dina collapsed into it, exhausted. She closed her eyes for a moment and then opened them, looking back towards the entrance of the restaurant.

"I take it we're not going to be alone?" Siren asked.

After a moment, Jeffrey emerged on the pier, walking down the steps into the restaurant. He had changed out of his usual biking jacket and was wearing a loose Mexican sort of blouse, which was a brave thing for a man to wear, but it suited him. When he introduced himself to Siren, she could barely contain the pleased look that she threw Dina.

"Oh my God," Siren said. "Am I interrupting a date?"

"I don't know if it's a date."

"Well, *I* thought it was a date," Jeffrey said.

Siren smiled. "Well, now it's a threesome. So." She leaned forward, flexing her tattooed arms. "Tell me about yourself."

Jeffrey rested his chin on his hands. "There's really not much to tell. I'm a general practice lawyer. I do a lot of real estate because this is just a place where everybody does a lot of real estate. I do a little bit of criminal."

"That's what he's mostly been helping me with," Dina added.

"I'll reserve comment on that because it's privileged information. But mainly I've been helping Dina with trying to sell her property."

"But he did bust me out of jail today," Dina said.

"My God." Siren's mouth hung open in shock.

Dina grimaced. "Yeah." Then she cleared her throat. "Look. You two are the ones I've been spending the most time with for the last week and I... I just wanted to share some things. I think maybe by sharing them I might get to understand them a little bit better. I shared them with my grandmother, but it's complicated."

They both nodded. Dina realized that a person might worry if a friend said something like this. She expected some leeway from Siren, but Jeffrey was brand new—and a genuinely good guy, acting like a friend already. So maybe it would be safe to say some craziness.

"Something really strange attacked Trent. And then when I put Trent into my car to take him to the hospital, it attacked me."

"What was it?" Jeffrey asked. He looked like he wanted to take out a pencil and start writing things down.

"I'm going to tell you, and I don't want you to think I'm crazy. I'm going to tell you what I saw."

"Okay," they both said. As in *get on with it*.

"Something… got into a Dominic Delvecchio doll. The real one, the one that we had stored in the museum. The best I can figure it it's some kind of… animal? I figure that, I say that, because I'm not the kind of person who would believe anything else. Some kind of animal. My grandmother thinks that it was something else, some kind of magic. But I'm going to go with animal, because this thing moved like an octopus that was wrapped in clothes. It *hurt* Trent. And then it was moving around in the car. And that's how I wrecked my car. And in the end, I wrapped it up in a duffel bag and I threw it in the reservoir."

"So that's it." She stopped, looking at both of them. And then she leaned back. She ran over what she had said thoroughly in her mind. There were no lies in it. It was a story that she could live with. "Do you guys believe me?"

Jeffrey sat back with his eyebrows up. Siren cleared her throat.

"You don't believe me?"

Jeffrey answered, "Well, the way you've presented it, I guess it's easy enough to believe. Except for that, I really don't know any animal that would be like that. But I mean if you say you got rid of it…"

"The craziest thing is it was dressed up like Dominic," Dina continued. A waitress came by, and they ordered mai tais. "I think my mother would feel like I'm being punished for losing my faith in it."

Siren said, "Honey, you don't know that, and you've been through a lot. Your poor mother."

"You know, I used to be *all* into it." Dina looked out at the ocean. Distantly, in her mind, she heard barbershop quartet music. "When I was a little kid, I knew every one of the songs that my great-grandfather would sing with Dominic. And when I was about eight years old, my mother got it in her head that she would open up the museum and bring in performers, you know, ventriloquists from around the state. This was around. I guess around 2000 or 2001. Around 9/11?"

The other two nodded, letting her go.

"So I told all my friends, and I invited them and everybody else from the school. And I went to the museum on Friday, and I waited. In the little movie theater, the video room where we show films about Dominic. And I had printed up sheets of music for people to sing all the songs. And I was so excited." Dina shrank in her seat, remembering the nothingness of sitting there in the little theater. "Nobody came. My family had dedicated their *lives* to this world. These songs, this concept of the culture. And we were convinced that it was important to *everybody*. And nobody came."

In her memory, she moved forward. "So when I graduated from high school, I changed my name to Maron, and I pretended that the family didn't exist. Anyway, I don't know what it was that injured Trent and attacked me. Maybe what I saw was just a hallucination exacerbated by grief. Maybe I need to see a doctor. Maybe it's just my family moving around in my subconscious, making me believe things. It's just so hard for me to believe… that Dominic would have power after all this time."

"An animal," Jeffrey said. "You said you decided to think of it as an animal."

"Of course."

"It doesn't matter," Siren said, grasping her hand. "It's at the bottom of a lake now, and that's good enough."

Dina smiled. They ordered fish tacos and moved on to other stories. Jeffrey had graduated law school around the same time as Dina. He had been briefly married to a law school sweetheart, but it hadn't really worked out. But there were no bad guys, no children.

"I have a seventeen-year-old daughter; she lives in Seattle with her mother," Jeffrey said. "I get to see her a few times a year. It's not really what

I preferred, but, yeah, no bad guys."

They finished off the dinner, and by the end of the evening, Dina, slightly buzzed, felt better about the whole thing. She felt so much saner than when she had been picked up at the police station. Siren made a big deal about letting them walk back to Jeffrey's car alone. She hugged Dina and said, "for what it's worth, I believe you. Whatever it is."

Jeffrey dropped her off at home, reached over to open the door, and she kissed him. He tasted like salt, and he was a good kisser.

Within a moment, wordlessly, she had convinced him to follow her up to her condo. The day had begun a disaster and ended in bliss.

Chapter 17
Saturday, February 12

DINA WOKE ON SATURDAY MORNING GLAD more than anything else that she was self-employed and didn't have anywhere to be. The first thing that happened before she even opened her eyes was to mentally think through her calendar, wondering when her first call was. It was a habit that went all the way back to law school, and one that still held with her. The mental calendar flipped over in her mind, and she remembered it was Saturday. And then she remembered Jeffrey and her eyes popped open. She could hear the wind outside the window. She sat up, looking to the side of the bed. There was no one there.

Well, that's just great, she thought. Already she was writing it all off. Jeffrey would disappear and she would probably never hear from him again. What was it about guys like this? All they wanted to do was get in your pants just once, what, just so they could say they could? *God damn it.*

Then she heard movement in the kitchen. Whatever embarrassment she felt about doubting that he was still there filtered away because, instead, there was somebody puttering around with pots and pans, and she couldn't imagine a more beautiful sound. She grabbed a terrycloth robe off the door and some slippers and walked out of the bedroom into the living area there the sun was blazing in. The bright sun always made her furniture look somewhat shabby, but she could live with it.

Jeffrey stood shirtless in the kitchen frittering with a frying pan. "Morning, sleepyhead."

She smiled.

"There is coffee. And I looked in your refrigerator, but all I could find was this turkey bacon. So I guess that's what you like?"

"Oh my gosh," she said. "Absolutely." And to think that she thought that he would be gone. She went over and kissed the back of his neck and reached around him to find an oven mitt and handed it to him. His eyes crinkled as he smiled.

As they had breakfast at her little table, Jeffrey told her about his own practice. "It's kind of embarrassing," he said. "I tell people that I hung out my own shingle because it's exciting or because I get to make my own hours. But the truth was I was perfectly in the middle of my graduating class and everybody else was getting all the internships with law firms, and I just couldn't be bothered. Or maybe you could say I just couldn't compete."

Dina shrugged. She knew exactly what Jeffrey was talking about. "Do you like what you do?"

"I like it well enough. It's not law firm hours. I have a boat at the marina, and I take it out whenever I get the chance. I get to bike around. I get to be here with you this morning. You're easily the best client I've had."

"I'll bet you say that to all the clients."

"Oh wow!" Jeffrey suddenly exclaimed, looking past her. "Is this another one of these dolls?" He got up and walked over to find the Dominic Delvecchio replica that she had sitting in her papasan chair. "So this is the thing that's been stalking you?"

"Sure," she said. Actually, it really did give her the heebie jeebies to have this store-bought version in her house now. If she hadn't been so exhausted over the last few days, she would have thought to throw it away. "Why don't you come back and have some more coffee."

He did come back, but he brought the Dominic dummy with him. It was propped on his arm, seated exactly the way that her great-grandfather always held the dummy. She looked in its eyes. This one's eyes, just like the real one, were curiously wet, which struck her as some kind of amazing technique. Jeffrey kept the dummy balanced on one arm while he reached out to fiddle with the trigger in the back of the doll's head. "He doesn't look like an animal to me!"

Dina was getting uncomfortable. "Can we not talk about it?" She was already feeling like the experiences with Dominic were some kind of dream that she had misunderstood, and she wasn't interested in revisiting them. And she was a little miffed that Jeffrey wasn't getting the hint.

"You don't want to talk about it?" He said, making the dolls mouth move.

Now that made her laugh. "You're supposed to keep your own lips from moving when you do that." He tried again, this time creating too little parted holes between his lips. She remembered that from taking ventriloquism lessons when she was a kid. Your first step, you were supposed to hold your lips together, letting them curl slightly so you had two open channels through your lips that you could speak out of. But the true masters, like her great-grandfather, showed no lip movement at all.

Jeffrey more or less admitted defeat. "Here, let me get you some coffee." He looked at the dummy and said to it, "Shall we get some coffee?"

It was amazing. People routinely found it impossible not to talk to a dummy when one was around. She wondered if that would be true of almost anything with eyes.

There was something flapping in the wind outside, and she glanced out at the balcony. That was when she realized that the sliding door was cracked slightly open. And more, that there was a broken straw hat blowing around outside against the bars of her balcony.

Over a puddle of water.

She was still staring at the balcony as she said, "Jeffrey, put that thing down."

"Put what thing down?" Came another voice, and it wasn't Jeffrey. It was something *like* Jeffrey, something like Jeffrey's voice. But it wasn't quite right. She turned around. The doll was wrapped around Jeffrey's shoulders, its wooden head perched next to Jeffrey's head. And it was using its coiled arm to hold Jeffrey's hand with a butcher knife up to Jeffrey's neck.

Chapter 18

"NO, NO, NO, PLEASE NO," SHE stammered, reaching out.

"Hit it, hit it with something," Jeffrey rasped. His free hand was reaching towards the counter,

The dummy spoke, its voice sounding slightly like Jeffrey's. "Move your hands not, stranger, or your life will be forfeit right here."

"Do you have a gun?" Jeffrey asked. His eyes were wide.

"Do you know what I think?" the doll said. Its voice was beginning to sound more like Jeffrey's with every word. "I think there's nothing worth living for. I think you have a terrible law practice. Doesn't he, Dina? Did he make a good companion? That is the only thing I can see. That is all I can imagine this person being good for. You remind me so much of my sibling that I grew up with. Who you look so much like."

At this last phrase, the dummy tilted its straw hatted head towards Dina. Then it went on. "I think he has nothing worth living for. He had a night with you and that was all that he could bear." And then, belaboring it no more, Jeffrey's hand slipped the knife across his own throat, and he collapsed as blood gushed across tile.

Dina stumbled backwards, covering her mouth as she tripped over her own coffee table and smashed into the floor. She heard a scuffling, and then the dummy bounded high and landed on the coffee table, perching, its four limbs curling as it bent its wooden head towards her. "There is no one for you but me. You have one week to accept this." She was speechless as it scuttled, loping, coiling its limbs inside of the cloth pants and jacket towards the glass door. It wriggled nearly its entire body through the crack and finally shoved the door open a little more to get its head through. Then it disappeared over the railing and towards the ocean.

"Jeffrey!" She screamed and crawled and then got up and ran to find him gasping on the floor. Gasping and then gasping less. She dialed 911 as she watched him die.

Chapter 19

THE PARAMEDICS WASTED LITTLE TIME TRYING to revive Jeffery because there was a puddle of blood covering her kitchen tiles that stretched from wall to wall. Dina stood far from them, could barely hear herself respond whenever they threw her a question. It was clear that Jeffrey was dead, clear that he had done it with a knife in his own hands. The police officers said the same thing. She did, however, hear one of the cops talking into a radio; the officer stopped to glance at her, and she knew what the guy must be saying. A line from an old movie came back to her, when an investigator realizes that a bunch of lawyers are being murdered: he says, "The lawyers at your firm sure are accident-prone." That was what was going on in her life right now. The people around her were *accident-prone.* Which never looked good for whoever they were accident-prone around.

A plain-clothed police officer, a woman with sad eyes and bleached blond hair pulled back in a ponytail, asked Dina questions while Dina stared out at the balcony.

"Did he indicate to you that he was going to do this?"

"No." She shook her head. There was nothing she could say. Nothing that would make sense.

Her phone was buzzing. She looked at it:

9773.

It took her a moment to remember that it was Jeffrey's number.

"Do you need somebody to stay with you? Do you need someone to sit with you?" the detective was asking.

The phone kept buzzing. The detective looked down and said, "Do you want to answer that?"

Dina finally nodded and picked up the phone from the coffee table, hit the green button and held it up to her ear. There was a long pause, and then she heard the ocean and traffic. And then, after a moment, she heard somebody that sounded just like Jeffrey, but not quite.

"You are running out of friends," it said. It was the dummy. It was Dominic. "I know of *one* other friend though, and I'm going to visit her now. If you want to come, you can be with me. Or I suppose you can destroy me, but I'm going to keep closing in on those you love."

She was listening to this, feeling tears coming to her eyes, tears and frustration and rage while the police officer looked at her patiently. The call clicked off. Dina put the phone down on the arm of her chair, and when she did, she was able to glance past the police officer and see, once again, the slick of blood and the madness of paramedics all over her kitchen.

One other friend.

"There is somebody I want to sit with," she said. "I can go see my friend. She's at the Hula Hut down the beach."

The police officer nodded politely. "I think it would be good if you got out of here."

The smell of blood was so strong in the kitchen that she nearly threw up as she passed it. She ripped the front door open and ran for Siren's restaurant.

Chapter 20

DINA STUMBLED OUT ONTO OCEAN HIGHWAY and ran for her rental car. But as she was reaching it, she looked down the highway and could see that traffic had been stopped for the festival festivities. It was only about a mile and a half to the Hula Hut, so she opted to grab her bicycle. There was a whole bunch of activity going on the main drag, starting at about the point of the Community Museum, all the way to the Governor's Cove neighborhood at the South End. Between that were all the boutiques and restaurants, all backing up to the ocean. And right now, Ocean Highway was crammed with crowds standing on the sidewalks and floats and parade personnel, people on unicycles, people with hula hoops. People juggling fire. Dina covered the first mile of the highway on her bike easily and then had to get off because she had reached the beginning of the parade and the crowd on the sidewalks.

The premiere attraction of the Mujeres Festival Parade was its art floats. Teams would spend six weeks or a couple of months building a float that perfectly recreated a famous work. She passed a tall float that recreated Picasso's *Guernica* with a number of actors in strange costumes that stretched their bodies, so they fit together, creating the cubist masterpiece. An even stranger effect was the next float that she passed, which recreated one of those paintings by an artist whose name she couldn't remember, where a person's face was built from different vegetables, the costumes inside of the stacks of onions and tomatoes. The arrangement made it difficult to see where the faces of the actual models were, which was part of the wonderful illusion about the art parade. But she wasn't here for that. Instead, she bashed against a tank-top wearing dude in nose-covering zinc. The guy cursed at her while his girlfriend looked her up and down. Dina must have looked like some kind of rage-crazed zombie smashing through people.

When she reached the restaurant, it was difficult to see in because it was so bright outside. But Siren was a silhouette that she recognized. From familiarity. Her friend was laying out menus and seating a family. "Siren!"

Siren looked up and nodded at her, and then turned her attention back to the family, probably giving them a spiel about how she would be right back then. Siren excused herself and sashayed up to the front. "Oh my God, what happened to you?"

Dina looked down and realized that she had speckled blood on her hands. Like maybe she had murdered someone.

"Come with me," Dina said urgently, dragging Siren to the edge of the restaurant and pulling her as best she could behind a plant. Any camouflage would be helpful.

"What's going on?" Siren demanded.

"It killed Jeffrey."

"What?"

"Yes." Dina. Nodded vigorously. "Jeffrey is dead. And you need to get someplace safe. It called me after it killed Jeffrey."

"It?"

"Come on!" Dina flounced. "You know what I'm talking about. *Dominic.* "

Siren stared at her, nodding, but not as though she was following what Dina was saying. It was obvious that this was just a step too far, something that Siren was not going to be able to believe. Just then, the door opened, and Dina looked past the plant to see two police officers enter. Maybe they were looking for her. Maybe they wanted to talk to her and decided that they shouldn't have let her leave her apartment. Or maybe they were just random cops. Dina said quickly, "You need to get someplace safe. Dominic knows you work here."

Dina headed out the side door and then back out to Ocean Highway, scanning for anywhere the dummy might come from. There was a fire truck passing by, recreating something that she was sure she had seen once in a Norman Rockwell collection. There was a fashion model dressed up as a little boy and another fashion model dressed up as a Dalmatian as they rode the fire truck of the Mujeres fire department. But perched high up on the folded ladder above the truck, Dina saw Dominic Delvecchio with a pair of scissors in his mouth.

Chapter 21

DINA RAN THROUGH THE POSSIBILITIES. IF Dominic was coming to kill Siren, maybe the dummy didn't know exactly where she was. Or maybe the creature was just playing with her because just now it looked down at her as she spotted it. At first, she was certain that Dominic was going to leap down and stab her. She could picture it all, how it would coil its arms around her shoulders and then slash into her neck with the scissors that it carried between its wooden teeth.

But the fire truck that it was riding kept moving, rolling down the highway, slowly pulling away from her. And then she became aware that the dummy was swiveling its wooden head looking for a target, and suddenly it stopped because it picked one—or rather two. There were a pair of surfer girls standing in front of Tony's Tex Mex, filming the parade with their phones. Both of them were pale somehow, even in the sun, both of them with long blonde hair and broad swimmers' shoulders. They must spend all of their time training indoors, but today they came out, and if they didn't know better, they were going to wind up with sunburns by the end of the day. But that didn't matter, because the dummy was about to leap and slash at least one of their throats. Dina ran fiercely towards the corner where the girls were standing. She started gibbering, not even hearing what she was saying. One of the girls brought up her phone to film Dina as she ran towards them, her arms extended. "Lookout!" she lowered her shoulders and slammed into one of the girls who knocked into the other. They banged their knees as the three of them stumbled and she heard one of them yell. "What the actual fuck?" Dina rose to her feet, holding out her hands, "I'm sorry. I'm sorry." She looked up at the fire truck. it was already past them. The dummy was gone.

A guy in the crowd nearby shouted, "What the fuck was that about?" There were cell phones being pointed at her. She was being turned into an Instagram meme. A candidate for office and now a random weirdo knocking people down in the street.

"I'm sorry! I thought somebody was going to jump off the—" And then she ran out of words, backing up.

"Dina!" came the voice of Siren.

Siren emerged from the crowd and grabbed Dina by the shoulders, and then moved swiftly with her. They turned down one of the side streets toward the fishing piers. When they reached some shade, Siren said, "Start over."

"It's real. It came back. It killed Jeffrey. Oh my God, it killed Jeffrey. I watched it happen. It made him slash his own throat." Tears came to her eyes. "And now it's coming after you!"

"Okay," Siren said. "So what do we do?"

Dina forced herself to calm down. "We need to talk to my grandmother. We need to get to the retirement home. She'll know what to do."

Chapter 22

WHEN THEY FOUND GRANDMA, SHE WAS in the bedroom of her little apartment. She took forever coming to the door. She appeared to have changed, aged overnight. She was using a cane and her hair wasn't properly kept. She hadn't done her makeup. Dina reflected that she wasn't used to seeing her grandmother look like a grandmother.

Gretchen obviously felt much the same way. "Jesus," the old woman said. "You look like I feel."

Dina and Siren helped Grandma sit on a loveseat.

"What's wrong?" Dina asked.

"I just don't have a lot of energy right now. What's happening?"

"It's gotten worse," Dina said. "The creature has a voice now. And a phone that it stole from my boyfriend. He doesn't have very dexterous fingers, but. It looks like he's able to make calls."

"Did he steal the voice from your boyfriend?"

"Yes."

Grandma nodded. "It's a thing that he can do. It's very hard not to try to talk for that thing."

Dina said, "You told me that I needed to take control of the dummy. But I didn't want to take control of it. Is there anything else that we can do? I mean are there any directions and how to deal with it? Has the dummy always been possessed?"

"That's a lot of questions," Grandma said. She took a long moment, and then she started wherever she wanted to. "You know, when your great-grandfather died, he left me about ten thousand dollars and left the dummy a quarter of a million dollars. Just to go into the maintenance of the museum —and the original house."

"I'm sorry, that sucks," Siren said.

"Oh, honey, I'm not mentioning it because I'm mad that my father didn't leave me any money. I mean, remember, by the time he died, I was already making a lot of money as a TV star. But it was so damn insulting. But anyway, I know that he left instructions for the maintenance of the original house, the one that we lived in back when we were in Saint Louis. I think if you wanted to find answers, you should go there."

And then she looked very gray.

"Are you okay?" Dina leaned forward. "Can I get you anything? Do I need to call the nurse?"

Grandma waved her off. "I just need to lay down." They helped her up. As she was going back into her bedroom, she stopped and said, "Stop that stupid thing. I'm tired of it being in our lives."

Chapter 23

Sunday, February 13

THE MIDDLE OF WINTER IS A terrible time to visit St. Louis, Missouri. As Dina tooled the rented SUV into the leafy neighborhood where her great-grandmother, grandfather and grandmother and Dominic had grown up. She felt the car occasionally slipping and sliding. The houses were beautiful, though, mostly white, gray, and smoky blue with extruding front porches. Because of the overcast, a homey glow of light from the inside spread out into the streets. It was the kind of neighborhood that people would always think of America representing, the kind that Walt Disney tried to capture with his Main Street USA at Disneyland.

Siren gave Dina directions from her phone, telling her which turns to take until they found their way to a little cul-de-sac. They parked in front of a hulking Victorian house, complete with a widow's walk.

Siren leaned forward. "So this is the home of Alan Bricker."

Dina nodded. "It's *bigger* than I expected."

The family lore of Bricker coming from nothing and building himself into an international star was somewhat offset in her mind now. As a little boy in the short pants of the turn of the century, Bricker would have been banging around in what was essentially a mansion.

But she also knew that the kind of money that Alan Bricker had generated absolutely dwarfed this sort of genteel American upper middle class. The Bricker Mansion had one of those front yards that sloped down from the front porch. And although the house appeared to be in good shape late in the afternoon, with a well-kept front yard, the sidewalk was tilted and cracked. Dina understood exactly what was going on. The town was not doing a very good job maintaining the right of way, such as the sidewalks. But her family's money was taking care of the yard.

There was ice and frost everywhere, and they stepped gingerly until they reached the top of the steps at the great wrap-around porch. They walked under a hanging shingle that said HISTORIC HOME TOUR AVAILABLE BY APPOINTMENT ONLY.

Siren went over and looked through the window. "Are we going to have to break in?"

Dina fished a key out of her pocket. "Of course not. You think we're going to climb in through the basement like the Scooby gang? You're forgetting that my grandma owns this place." She tried the different keys Grandma had given her until one of them worked the lock. She swung the door open and slid into the past.

Chapter 24

ALTHOUGH IT WAS FREEZING OUTSIDE, THE sturdy old house was well maintained and toasty warm. Inside, Dina found that she could open her coat and let the coolness surround her body as she surveyed the fake plants in great stone planters in the foyer. She tried to picture her grandmother wandering around this place as a toddler, but the way that she always really remembered Gretchen Bricker was the way she had mostly been photographed, as a teenage fashion model in 1960s wearing stockings and big flowery hats. How ravishing she would have been walking through this house, coming down from her bedroom upstairs. Dina and Siren walked to the back of the foyer and found themselves in a large kitchen.

The simple kitchen was done up in white. Older kitchens were never very exciting—there was some point in the late 20th century when suddenly people started making kitchens a fun place to hang out, but this one looked more like a place of torment. The kitchen had one of those rolling wooden islands and some equipment, but it was the opposite of a spot where you'd spend time on purpose.

"There's a coffee maker!" exclaimed Siren.

Dina nodded. "We're gonna be here awhile. You wanna make some?"

"I do, but let's see what we find first," Siren suggested. They went around the staircase and found a drawing room and a little den and the library, which turned out to be huge. With its enormous shelves, great, fluffy chairs, and large, wooden desk, the library had obviously served as an office for her great-grandfather.

Dina made the executive decision that they'd locate themselves here and Siren went to put the coffee on.

When Siren brought the coffee back, Dina was curled up in chair and staring at the Victorian bric-a-brac lining every surface. She took the coffee cup Siren handed her. "I could just curl up and stay here."

"It's not really my scene," Siren said. "But I get it."

It was starting to snow outside the window. Dina got up and went over to a shelf with a number of books that looked exactly alike. She read out the titles. *The Encyclopedia Catholica. The Encyclopedia Judaica.* Magical sourcebooks. "You know, I admit I don't really know what we're looking for." They used Post-its to flag encyclopedia entries on ventriloquist dummies. They did find a history of ventriloquism, but they didn't find anything that would make sense out of the creature that was Dominic Delvecchio.

Dina sat down for a moment, thinking of what her grandmother had said. *Do you know that doll had its own room?*

Finally she said, *"I* think we need to look at Dominic's room."

They moved from the foyer up the stairway until they reached an upper hall with a master bedroom at one end and three kids' bedrooms. One of them was not used at all. One appeared to be a shrine to Gretchen Bricker not unlike the fake bedroom back at the museum. And one, when they walked into it, was clearly the home of an immortal child.

"My God," Siren said. "It's like the Temple of Archie Andrews." There was a regular bed with blankets in a cowboy motif, images of lariats and cowboy hats, Tom Mix and Roy Rogers. On the walls hung pennants of the Oakland A's and the Saint Louis Cardinals.

"I wonder." Dina moved from desk to shelf, looking at the countless comic books and children's books, which surely were never read by anybody. "How did this work? *Did* it actually work? If you were Alan Bricker and you came in from one of your trips, you kissed your wife good night, you walked up the stairs and you put your *ventriloquist dummy* to bed. Did you tuck him in? Did you convince yourself that he *enjoyed* looking at these pennants?"

She walked around by the window, looking out to see icicles clinging to trees. Out in the cold, a boy in earmuffs was walking a great furry dog down the frozen sidewalk. Next to the window was a bulletin board with a variety of clippings about Alan Bricker and Dominic Delvecchio. The clippings reminded Dina of the chatter of the mannequins back at the museum, about the young ventriloquist Alan Bricker, and how he was impressing everybody in town. Indeed, there was an image here, a clipping of Alan as a teenager wowing the Boy Scouts. But what caught her eye just now was something that preceded even that. It said KAR KASTER TAKES SCOUTS UNDER HIS WING. It was an article dated August 20th, 1909.

All the boys were properly chuffed this week as at the VFW Hall. The local troop of Boy Scouts were treated to a demonstration of ventriloquist feats by none other than Kardamom Kastor, a world-famous thrower of voices.

Pictured below the article was a photograph of one of the scouts and the famous ventriloquist, so-named Kardamom Kastor, whose own ventriloquist dummy was wearing a white tuxedo. According to the caption, this doll was called Sam the Swami. The Boy Scout was Alan Bricker.

"Look at this," Dina said, tapping the bulletin board. "Alan is quoted as saying, 'I have been invited to go listen to a meeting of illusionists because I am so amazed by Kastor the Magnificent.'"

"He'll make an excellent apprentice," the magnificent one said. "This young man showed amazing skill during our ventriloquism demonstration."

Over next to the dresser, Siren gasped. "Check this out." She picked up and showed to Dina a thick, gold-painted candlestick. It was engraved:

To the Great Alan, From the Illusionist Servants of Sethlagore.

Dina shook her head. "What the hell is Sethlagore?"
"I'm not sure," Siren said. "But I know where to look."

"Good. This room gives me the creeps."

They took the Candlestick back downstairs to the Bricker Library. Dina started with *The Encyclopedia Judaica*. She looked up the name. SETHLAGORE.

"The spirit or angel over voices," she said. "Ah." There was a photograph of a seated stone statue on a work bench with the caption:

STATUE, SETHALAGORE, BRITISH MUSEUM, 1879.

And below that, in parentheses:

(Lost.)

They decided to get some of the coffee. They went back into the kitchen, Siren still carrying the ornamental candlestick in one hand while Dina carried the encyclopedia. The kitchen was one of those that had a swinging door and if you pulled it back it could really whip. When Dina went through a little fast, it caught Siren in the arm and the candlestick she was carrying rattled.

"I think there's something inside this thing." Siren shook the plaster candlestick like a maraca.

Dina put down the encyclopedia. She looked around and realized that there was no one to be disappointed any more. Over life, she had been the kind of person who cleaned up messes and who put things away. And in fact, except for the Dominic Delvecchio doll in her papasan chair, there was nothing ever out of place in her apartment. She was not the kind of person who would take a candlestick and deliberately lift it over her head and smash it to the floor. But when she did, it burst, sending shards scattering across the floor.

They knelt down. At the center of all of the plaster pieces was an old cloth, folded and refolded, bounded up with the rusty gold chain of an ancient rabbit's foot.

"This is something a kid would do," Siren said. "You have something you're hiding in a special place, and you wrap it in your lucky charm."

Dina slid the cloth out of the chain and opened it up. The cloth—she thought of it as a handkerchief—shined, pearlescent and shimmery in the light of the kitchen. When they unrolled it, it was as long as a scarf, and it had writing on it in dark purple script:

This and no other will bind thy gift forever, but take heed, Christian: all the talents will be lost and to stone Sethlagore will return.

Chapter 25

DINA SLAPPED THE HANDKERCHIEF, FOR THAT was the way she thought of it, down on the island in the middle of the kitchen.

She took out her phone and dialed the retirement community. "Hi there? I'm calling for Gretchen Bricker. Is she there? This is her granddaughter."

It was Tracy on the line. They chatted for a bit about how Dina had come to Gretchen's childhood home in Saint Louis.

"Well... she's had kind of an episode," Tracy said. "But I think she's doing a little bit better. She's still pretty out of it."

"An episode," Dina repeated. "Oh, God... like a stroke?"

"A minor one, yes."

Dina's chest flooded. She hated hearing that. As far as she was concerned, there was no such thing as a *minor* stroke.

Tracy went on, "But she really is doing a lot better, and I wouldn't tell you that if it wasn't true."

"Okay. Okay." Dina couldn't think of what else to say. "I'll come visit as soon as I'm back."

Siren handed Dina a cup of coffee, and Dina leaned against one of the counters. She looked across the kitchen, out the window at the cold gray day as the coffee steamed her face and nodded at the handkerchief. "So this is what we need."

"Do you want to talk about your grandmother?"

"Not really. Let's take care of this first. This handkerchief is what you have to bind it with. According to what it says, these illusionists gave Alan Bricker some kind of talent, and he took that talent and he got himself this ventriloquist dummy, and he bound that talent with it. He was given a way out, which is this handkerchief. To bind it. But for some reason he never used it."

"Why do you think that is?" Siren asked.

"I don't know. Maybe Alan was so arrogant that he couldn't imagine that his career would ever be at an end, or that anybody would ever want to do something different than what the great Alan Bricker wanted to do." She was thinking about how when Dominic was put into the glass box, his eyes were covered… but with an ornamental kerchief that had nothing to do with the magic at all. It was like he had been put on pause. Like Alan really did believe that maybe Gretchen would change her mind and become a ventriloquist, or maybe somebody in the family down the line… and that somehow, their use of the dummy would reflect back on the Great Alan Bricker.

She stuffed the shimmery handkerchief into her coat. True to her nature, she then grabbed a broom and swept up the pieces of the candlestick, neatly gathered them and put them into the trash. And then they hurried out, locked up behind them, and raced to the airport.

Chapter 26

DINA FOUND HERSELF LISTENING TO THE sounds of her own footsteps as she got back to the condo. Maybe she was looking for some comfort in their uniformity, or maybe she just didn't want to focus on anything else. She let herself in, and as soon as the door fell closed, she shut her eyes. She knew she wasn't done. Knew there was something she was waiting for. And a still kind of quiet echoed through the small living space, not even disturbed by Dina's own breath.

And just after the sun went down over her balcony, the phone rang. She was met with the stolen voice she'd come to despise.

"Are you ready, sister?"

Dina cringed and bit her lip as she clutched the phone.

His voice was sing-songy, and a not-quite perfect imitation of a human as he urged her, "Time to come claim me! Maybe just die trying… but if you don't come here, who knows? I just might destroy everything you love. Starting with that old sister of mine."

Listening behind the voice, Dina noticed some subtle clanking sounds. Distant, but distinct ones she identified immediately. They were the sounds of a marina.

The voice, Jeffrey's voice, was coming from the Mujeres Marina, and Jeffrey's boat.

Nestled between the restaurant piers and pleasure beaches to the north and the steep cliffs of Governor's Cove to the south, the Mujeres Marina sparkled like a jewel at night, the boats bumping and clanking in the piers with a gentle breeze.

Jeffrey Green's thirty-foot Sea Ray Sundancer, so identified because it was the background of several of his Facebook selfies, glowed like a tall, white ghost against a slip about 4 from the northern edge of the marina. There was no problem picking it out. As Dina parked her bike and walked down the pier, hew stomach twisting in knots, she wished that she had brought some kind of weapon—but what would she use? She couldn't very well shoot the dummy. No, she would have to wrestle with it again.

As she reached the boat, she looked up and caught a silhouette of someone small inside the cockpit. And then it was gone.

She grabbed the metal ladder and began to climb and heard the distant whistling of the dummy. She had no idea it could whistle, but as she dropped onto the deck near in the cockpit area, she recognized the tune. *Meet me tonight in dreamland.*

There was a ladder down to the cabin but for a moment she studied her surroundings, which glowed with the stars and the lights of the marina. Jeffrey clearly kept his boat set up for a deck party, and it touched her painfully to think he might have had a circle of friends eager for his next get-together. She saw a small fridge, cases of beer, some fishing nets. She didn't see fishing equipment, though. Maybe he brought it with him every time. Maybe he didn't fish.

"Is that you, sister?" came the voice that was Jeffrey's and not Jeffrey's. "Welcome aboard."

Slowly Dina began down the ladder, descending into darkness.

It was like a lounge down here. Wooden walls and a huge coffee table with a wide, cushy booth. A microwave and stovetop, coffee maker. On one wall, the fishing equipment. Lures and knives and something else that caught her eye before she moved on.

On the other wall hung a fifty-inch television, which was enormous for this space.

The dummy was turned away from her, seated on the little coffee table.

He was looking at the snowy TV screen, so that the snow enveloped his head.

"We lived in images," he said. "We lived by being seen. That was all we wanted. To take this snow and fill it with images that you people would *adore*."

Dina didn't answer. She wasn't about to debate with a demon.

"There is no mystery here," the dummy said as it turned towards her. "You know what I can do."

Yes. Yes, she did.

"This whole thing is way more complicated than it has to be," Dominic said. For a moment Dina was amazed that something about the way the dummy said that in Jeffrey's voice, it was though among Dominic's skills was the mimicry not just of voice but style, and maybe worse, maybe something deeper. The dummy stood and turned around, revealing a long, silvery fish-boning knife in a coiled arm.

"All *I* have to do is gut you! If I did that, then I could go away forever." He waggled his little wooden head, and his eyes grew wide as he whipped the knife to the side. Like this was all annoyingly *obvious*. He raised one of his undulating arms to the brim of the straw hat he wore. The dummy shook its head. "Why don't I? Because you and I can be siblings. Gretchen was my sibling, even though she rejected me. Your mother, Lorelei, never wanted to be. But you *could* be. Or you could die, and I won't be bound up again. And for the life of me I don't know why I *can't choose*."

Dina's eyes darted around. "What do you want?"

"I want *you* to choose."

"If it's up to me, you can go to Hell."

"Then I guess killing you it is." The dummy clacked and hissed then, *ack-ack-ack* as he leapt with the boning knife. He landed on the sofa next to the ladder, his knife plunging into the sofa cushion.

Dina grabbed something she had spotted off the wall as she clambered back up the ladder. It was a harpoon gun.

She reached the cockpit and heard it close behind her, turned to find her best possible shot, right now, with him exposed coming out of the hatch. She pulled the trigger on the harpoon gun and watched the bolt fly. It caught Dominic's hat and obliterated the old Styrofoam, but the dummy kept coming.

Dina turned around and looked for the ignition. She was getting rid of this thing whether she went with it or not.

I'm going to beat you. I'm going to beat you and cover your eyes and dump you deep.

She found the selector switch and hit the ignition and felt the boat rumble to life. She felt it tug on the mooring line and turned around just as the dummy came swiping at her with the boning knife, smacking into the leather seatback of the captain's chair.

Dina took the moment that it was wrestling with the knife to push past it and out onto the deck. She had to search, following around to the other side, to find the mooring lines. She was still holding the harpoon gun, but it was useless now and she let it drop.

The mooring line was tugging against a metal capstan. She couldn't free it. She spun around, searching, until her eyes rested on the bulkhead where Jeffrey had secured a fire axe, long, with a heavy black blade and a long spike end.

She yanked it free from the metal clasps that held it and wasted no time swinging it at the mooring line, once, twice and the line sailed free. She felt the boat start to churn out to sea.

"Family makes us stronger," Dominic said as she spun around to see him. Insane, how the voice emerged from inside its jaws. Magical and insane.

She wanted to scream *we are not family* in its face, but she didn't. It wouldn't be entirely true. "How can you say that and threaten Gretchen?" She asked, her voice sharp.

"She's not my sister anymore. She renounced me. She's still going to have to pay."

How hard is this? All I have to do is get you stuck somewhere and get a damn handkerchief around your eyes.

She ran straight for the dummy, swinging the axe. He bounced out of the way but hit a corner of the pilot house and she swung again, and this time she caught him with the spike of the axe. It connected with almost no dummy flesh but pierced right through Dominic's underarm, holding his shirt fast.

The dummy began whipping in a frenzy, his arms and legs undulating inside the cloth. She let go of the axe and pulled the handkerchief out of her back pocket and approached its head. It snapped at her fingers and then got its tentacles around her throat. She gasped and then she heard a *rip* as it tore free and sprang of the wall, wrapping its limps around her and biting hard at her shoulder.

She screamed in pain as they fell back, and she collided with something metal and then she was falling.

For a split second she tore her mind away from Dominic's mouth gnawing into her shoulder to realize they had crashed right over the ladder gate and the two of them were headed for the water.

Time slowed to a crawl as she hit the water and the only blessed stroke of luck was that the impact tore its mouth away from her shoulder. But it was wrapped around her, and they tumbled in the water next to the boat, which was slowly pounding past them.

She coughed and Dominic ratcheted out an *ack-ack-ack* at her and she kicked and dove as deep as she could.

Under the water there was dim light from the hull, and she forced her eyes open. Dominic's arms were slimy and strange under the cloth. She pushed against its chest with her left hand. Her lungs were starting to burn. It bit at her fingers and missed, and she brought up the handkerchief, looping it around its head, missing and coming down to its shoulders. It whipped its painted head, and she made a knot and then fainted towards it, and it bit at her shoulder again, and she elbowed it in the chin. Then she brought the handkerchief up and pulled the loop tight, covering its eyes.

Now it started to panic. She thought she heard it try to speak but what it wanted most was to get its eyes free and it gave up holding her and reached for the cloth. But she pulled it tight and looped it around again and tied it.

Something burst within it, a cloud of black gas beneath the water. But it was shaking, not fighting. She held it by the armpits and swam for the surface, her lungs crying out, until her head burst through the waves, and she gasped for air.

She floated there in the water with the dummy growing heavier.

The waves lapped at her head, and she spit out salt water. She needed to swim. The boat was long gone.

The dummy started to shake in her hands, trembling, and the slimy tentacles underneath its sleeves grew heavy.

It spat out bile underneath its covered face.

Ack-ack-ack.

And then the bile on its face began to congeal and harden. It fought to speak—no, to sing.

"Meet me tonight in dreamland—under the silvery moo…n…"

And then it was as heavy as stone, and she felt it taking her and she let it go.

Dina treaded water and looked down, and she caught the shimmer of its little patent leather shoes disappearing into the deep. Then she turned and swam back toward the marina.

Chapter 27
One week later

THEY GATHERED ON THE BALCONY OF Gretchen Bricker's apartment at the retirement center. Gretchen sat in a big, comfortable chair next to Dina. It was cool enough that it was nice to have a blanket over her and Dina decided it was worth having her own blanket. Siren got one too, and they sat there like three bugs all snuggled up.

Grandma wasn't speaking much. Dina was doing the talking.

"I felt," she said, "in those final moments, that being destroyed was what it really wanted. I don't think Dominic ever really wanted to *kill* me. I think it somehow just hoped that I would finally change my mind and want it to be part of my life." She looked at her grandmother. "Do you think that was true for you as well?"

Gretchen took a long moment and finally said, "I can't explain what causes people to think that we're suddenly going to change. Dominic never appeared to me the way that he did to you. But I know the sentiment. I think my father couldn't imagine a world where Alan Bricker was not the central idea on everybody's lips. He couldn't imagine a world where his daughter wouldn't want to make his world the center of hers."

Siren shook her head. "All this talk about how much Alan wanted to control everybody. Do you think that he was poisoned by the needs of the demon?"

Gretchen shook her head. "I wish, but no. Like finds like. I think loneliness and arrogance feed off one another."

They sat quietly for a while and finally, Dina said, "Well... I think I'm going to keep the museum. Learning about culture isn't going to kill anybody. Maybe it doesn't have to be so *Alan Bricker*-oriented. I wanted to start the tearoom; maybe I should get going on that." She stretched and got up and started folding the blanket.

Gretchen asked, "Where are you off to now?"

"I have an event at the public library. I'm still running for City Council. But you know what? I think I might change my name. Maybe I didn't want to be associated with Alan Bricker. But it's *your* name too. And that's just as powerful."

Sink with us, though.

A mile and a half off Mujeres, California, the water is a thousand feet deep, deeper than any diver typically will go, though it can be done. At a thousand feet, the hardened, sleeping creature that has grown accustomed to calling itself Dominic sleeps, covered in silt, nudged only occasionally by scuttling crabs and sea stars. Its shirt is tattered, and its garters grow black, but its shoes shine in the dark. It dreams fitfully and thinks it is Dominic, it dreams of the little room with the pendants, it dreams of ancient times. It dreams of seafloor worms that crawl on its face, and it dreams, or perhaps it knows, that they are finding its blindfold, and finding it very tasty.

CASTLE BRIDGE MEDIA RECOMMENDS...

If you liked this book, you might also enjoy reading the following titles from Castle Bridge Media available on Amazon or by order at your favorite book store:

Animal Charmer
By Rain Nox

Austinites
By In Churl Yo

Bloodsucker City
By Jim Towns

THE CASTLE OF HORROR ANTHOLOGY SERIES
Volume 1
Volume 2: *Holiday Horrors*
Volume 3: *Scary Summer Stories*
Volume 4: *Women Running From Houses*
Volume 5: *Thinly Veiled: The 70s*
Volume 6: *Femme Fatales**
Volume 7: *Love Gone Wrong*
Volume 8: *Thinly Veiled: The 80s*
Volume 9: *Young Adult*
Volume 10: *Thinly Veiled: Saturday Mournings*
Edited By Jason Henderson and In Churl Yo
*Edited By P.J. Hoover

Castle of Horror Podcast Book of Great Horror: Our Favorites, Top Tens and Bizarre Pleasures
Edited By Jason Henderson

Dream State
By Martin Ott

Dominic
By Lee Guzman

FRENCH DECEPTION
A Forgery in Paris
By Janice Nagourney

FuturePast Sci-Fi Anthology
Edited by In Churl Yo

GLAZIER'S GAP
Ghosts of the Forbidden
By Leanna Renee Hieber

The Hermes Protocol
By Chris M. Arnone

Isonation
By In Churl Yo

Junk Film: Why Bad Movies Matter
By Katharine Coldiron

MID-LIFE CRISIS THRILLERS
18 Miles From Town
By Jason Henderson
Lost Angel
By Sam Knight

Nightwalkers: Gothic Horror Movies
By Bruce Lanier Wright

THE PATH
The Blue-Spangled Blue
By David Bowles
The Deepest Green
By David Bowles

SURF MYSTIC
Night of the Book Man
By Peyton Douglas
Dark of the Curl
By Peyton Douglas

Yesterday's Tomorrows: The Golden Age of Science Fiction Movies
By Bruce Lanier Wright

Please remember to leave us your reviews on Amazon and Goodreads!

THANK YOU FOR SUPPORTING INDEPENDENT PUBLISHERS AND AUTHORS!

castlebridgemedia.com